Murder Manor

A Psychological and Paranormal Thriller

Cori Nevruz

MASONBORO PRESS

Masonboro Press. LLC

For my Book Bitch, Leslie Brunt.

CHAPTER ONE

Ella Whitmore

OCTOBER 2024

I'm going to die.

Ella Whitmore stood with her back against her closed bedroom door as a tear fell down her flushed cheek. She'd found what she was looking for—the information needed to break her story wide open and finally make a name for herself.

As she'd sorted through the papers hidden under the closet floor, she'd let her mind spin, dreaming of her future and of the possibilities. Ella would be the biggest name in journalism, but it wouldn't stop there. She would be a celebrity, could maybe become a contestant on a reality TV show. Take her 15 minutes of fame and turn them into a career.

But as the information she'd discovered sank in, she realized she was in danger. Without putting anything back where she found it, she sprinted back down the hall to her bedroom, only to find him staring up at her from the base of the stairs.

Returning to her room, Ella secured the door and sat on the edge of her bed and stared out of the window. Her time was coming to an end. The room was shrouded in darkness, illuminated only by a thin sliver of moonlight cutting through the gloom. Her mind raced as she tried to concoct a plan to ensure that no matter what happened to her, that her story got out. In what were surely her final moments, her mind was clear and her emotions held at bay. If she opened her door and tried to run, he would catch her. With no wifi or cellular service atop the mountain, she couldn't send the photos of what she found. She thought of hiding her phone which held the indisputable proof or even tossing it out the window for someone to find. But, the man wasn't an idiot. When he was done with her, he would find her phone one way or another.

She placed her shaking hand down on the bed beside her, where it brushed against her journal. Flipping to a random page and using the light from her phone she frantically jotted down the main incriminating points, then stuffed the journal between the mattress and the box spring. She sat up once again, an uneasy calm washing over her body, just as her phone flickered off. The battery was dead, and there was no point in charging it now. Her time was up.

Though the inky blackness of the room dulled her vision, her awareness of the surrounding sounds was heightened—she could hear nothing over the steady rhythm of her heartbeat.

A new sound echoed through the room—a faint metallic click. Ella turned toward the source of the noise. A slice of moonlight cut across the timeworn, hardwood plank floors, and up the solid, oak door. Her eyes followed the path up the door to the ancient brass lock and to the aged, discolored knob above it. The rickety antique chair wedged under the doorknob wouldn't offer much protection, but it served as one more barrier between her and her hunter.

The metallic click echoed again, and this time she saw the doorknob begin to turn. There was no point in trying to be quiet anymore. He had come for her. Hiding was no longer an option—all she could do now was fight or flee.

With a sudden surge of determination, she jumped up. Abandoning any pretense of silence, the jiggling of the doorknob intensified, growing louder and more insistent. With a quick tug, she grabbed the bed sheets in handfuls and tore them from the mattress, praying she had enough time to fashion a make-shift rope.

She pressed her face against the cold windowpane, desperate to see what lay below her unfamiliar, temporary lodging. Her frantic breath fogged the glass creating an opaque cloud which she wiped away with her shirt sleeve. The room was on the second floor, but given that the lodge was built on the edge of a mountain, the drop from the window to the ground was at least fifty feet.

The sound of the free-spinning doorknob was soon accompanied by heavy banging against the door. The locking mechanism beneath the knob wouldn't hold out much longer.

As she considered her escape options, she realized that even if she managed to anchor the sheet to the bedpost, the drop would be lethal. The leaves only partially covered the ground, leaving the jagged rocks below exposed.

Frustrated, she sank back onto the bed, banging the heels of her palms against her temples, desperately trying to conjure another idea. But once again, she froze. The noise from the other side of the door had stopped.

Was he gone? Had he breached the room and was now standing over her—waiting for her to open her eyes?

Taking a deep breath, she let an involuntary whimper escape her lips. Summoning her courage, she lowered her hands and turned to face the door. To her relief, there was no looming figure waiting to pounce— the door remained closed, the chair wedged under the knob.

She tiptoed around the bed, pausing only when her foot pressed down on a floorboard that creaked in protest. After standing motionless for a moment, teeth clenched and one eye squeezed shut, she moved closer to the door. Leaning forward, she turned her head and pressed her ear against the wood. Silence enveloped her, and as she remained motionless. Her eyes scanned the room, as if tuning her hearing to the frequency of the unfamiliar room.

She let her right hand lower to the doorknob. It was cold against her skin, sending goosebumps rising along her arm. She began to turn the knob when a deafening crash echoed through the lodge. Panic surged through her body, and she released the door. She jumped backward, swinging her arms and kicking wildly, inadvertently knocking the chair off its back legs and onto its side. Staring down at the spindly, old chair she had desperately used as a barricade, she came to the realization that the noise she'd heard hadn't come from the hallway outside her room—it came from downstairs.

Acting on instinct, she seized what might be her only chance to escape—kicking the chair aside, flipping the lock, and yanking the door wide open. She dashed down the stairs, reaching the first floor in seconds, and burst through the front door. She crossed the porch and leaped down the steps to the driveway.

Her only thought as she sprinted down the stairs from her room was *escape,* but as her bare feet hit the sharp gravel of the driveway and pain shot through her legs, her mantra shifted to simply: *run.*

The gravel drive ended at a road that wound down the mountain to the town below, but no matter how fast she ran, it seemed to stay just out of reach.

When she finally reached the road, she allowed herself a glance over her shoulder. She expected to see a dark figure bearing down. Her active imagination led her to expect her pursuer to be chasing her, wielding a rusty axe or sharp blade glinting in the glare of moonlight. What she didn't expect was a clear view of the mountain lodge at the end of an empty driveway.

She leaned forward, hands on her knees, and took a few deep breaths. She wanted to sit and check her shredded feet, but knew that if she let herself rest, she'd never be able to stand again.

Walking through the woods would offer more cover when he inevitably came after her, but straying from the road meant risking getting lost - and possibly encountering a dangerous animal. *Another dangerous animal,* she thought. It wasn't long before the pain in her feet began to catch up with her. Since no one seemed to be chasing her, she drifted to the middle of the road, where the painted center lines were easier on her sore feet than the cracked asphalt.

The town was miles down the mountain, but as long as she kept moving, she'd make it there eventually.

A deep, menacing growl echoed through the night, and she was grateful she'd stayed on the road. As the roar intensified, she spun around, trying to figure out where the approaching noise was coming from. It wasn't until the sudden glare of headlights from an all-terrain vehicle lit up the darkness that she realized she wasn't being hunted by a wild animal, but by a monster in human form.

Her aching feet forgotten, she bolted toward the side of the road. If she could make it across the shallow ditch and into the trees, she could disappear into the cover of the forest. At least then, he'd be forced to chase her on foot.

With her eyes locked on the treeline, she pushed herself to run faster, her body straining for the safety mere feet away. But before she could reach her refuge, the man leapt from the ATV, slamming her to the ground. Her head hit the frozen earth with a painful thud.

She felt a resigned sense of relief as darkness closed in, her attacker's hands encircling her neck and a sinister smile spreading across his face.

CHAPTER TWO

Rachel Johnson

NOVEMBER, 2024

Rachel felt as if she might explode. The first five hours of the drive west was bad enough. Her dad sat in the driver's seat, singing along with the radio and butchering lyrics to her favorite songs with wild abandon. Her mom sat rigid in her seat, her forced smile betraying her irritation as she held back comments on his distracted driving to avoid sparking an argument in the tight confines of their car. Even in the back seat, Rachel had not a sliver of peace, leaning against the window to escape the flailing limbs of her sleeping siblings.

But after a pit stop in the tiny rural town to grab a few last-minute supplies before heading up the mountain, Rachel's 14-year-old brother, Tenner was wide awake and buzzing with excitement—fidgeting between his two sisters.

"Can we go snowboarding?"

"Am I allowed to explore the mountain?"

"Do you think we'll see a bear?"

Rachel watched her mom's eye twitch in the visor mirror and mouthed a silent prayer that her dad would quit humming before her mom reached over, grabbed the wheel, and sent them all plummeting over the mountain's edge.

"Polar bears are the only bear species that actively hunts to kill humans," Mia announced in her usual deadpan tone.

At fifteen, Mia was only a year and a half younger than Rachel, but the two couldn't be more different. While Rachel was recognized by many (and envied) as the teacher's pet, Mia's black-lined lips were more accustomed to speaking of darkness and decay than anything else. Her random, often disturbing facts had a strange way of showing up at the perfect moment to defuse tension—or deflect attention away from an awkward situation.

Years ago, their mom put the sisters in a community theater production. Mia worked behind the scenes with the stagehands, while Rachel's character, *Brainy Student 3*, had one measly line. But when her big moment came, she froze, forgetting all five words. Sensing her sister's panic, Mia stepped from backstage and into the spotlight, announcing to the audience, "Eating boogers can boost your immune system."

And just like that, in her own quirky way, Mia had saved the day. Now, years later, Mia sat in the backseat with her head against the window, watching as her random fact dissolved the tension in the car, confusion settling over everyone's faces.

Rachel couldn't help but notice the stark difference between their smooth highway drive and the rough road winding up to the mountain lodge. More than once, her dad had to swerve around massive potholes or steer clear of the crumbling edges of the narrow shoulder. The constant jostling was uncomfortable enough without Tenner's sweaty body bouncing into hers. He only recently started needing to wear deodorant—and hadn't yet mastered the habit of actually applying the product.

Rachel took a deep breath through her mouth, squeezing her eyes shut, hoping the erratic movement wouldn't make her sick. A heavy sigh escaped her lips—thinking about how none of them wanted to be there. Tenner would rather be with friends, Mia would certainly opt to sit alone in her dark room over being jammed in the back seat like sardines, and Rachel had college applications to prepare. Her dad started humming again, and though Tenner and Mia both rolled their eyes and their mom's fists clenched tighter, Rachel felt a smile tug at her lips. His humming was annoying, and when he sang, his lyrics were always wrong—but he would make the most of their family time together. There wasn't a universe in which he would have chosen a vacation in an old mountain lodge. But here he was—without complaint—because his wife had asked. The two of them had been through a lot together, high school sweethearts who'd weathered every storm. Rachel and her siblings had heard the story countless times: their mom had stood by their dad when he needed her most, and he'd never stopped feeling indebted to her. This was her world now, and he was just along for the ride.

CHAPTER THREE

Ella Whilmore

LATE SEPTEMBER, 2024

Ella's scheduled interview with a well-known gang leader in Atlanta was supposed to be her big break. She'd followed a lead, and found what she then thought would be the story of the century. Had her superiors known what she was looking into, they would've pulled her off, putting a more seasoned journalist on the story. But, Ella found the link and she wanted the story. And if she was being honest with herself, she wanted the credit. She was tired of doing all the work for senior co-workers to swoop in and take all the glory. It was her turn to become the story.

Unfortunately, on her way to the meeting, she was grabbed from behind and tossed in a van only to find out she'd been kidnapped by an FBI task force that was watching the gang. Her interview would've put an undercover agent at risk of being exposed as well as risking the three year investigation. After the embarrassing undressing she received from her boss for taking unnecessary risks and not following protocol, she was put on a 30-day leave, where she would be required to take online safety and journalism ethics classes from her laptop.

Rather than wasting another day pacing her claustrophobic studio, Ella slammed her laptop shut, tossed it in a backpack, and slipped behind the wheel of her aging coupe. She pointed it north, toward the shadowed mountains of North Carolina—toward the one person she still knew up there. Her roommate from college was still in school working towards an advanced degree, buried in coursework and caffeine, but Ella didn't care. The mandated class videos could drone on from anywhere.

The welcome was warm enough. But by the second day, the apartment felt lonely. Her friend vanished into a routine of lectures and late nights, leaving Ella to drift through long hours on her own.

Enjoying the crisp mountain air and welcoming both the change of seasons and the start of a new school year, Ella sat on the patio of a university café with her laptop, ready to tackle yet another day of often-ignored journalism ethics. Though summer wasn't technically over as far as dates go—the cool morning had more students in jeans than shorts. The steady stream of fresh-faced undergrads—heading to class, discovering independence, testing boundaries—proved distracting.

Ella had only been out of school a year, and while she didn't miss it, it somehow felt like a lifetime ago. At the table to her right, a cute college couple had settled in. From the conversation she couldn't help but overhear, the girl was a freshman, just starting out, while the guy carried himself with the ease of a seasoned student. The girl radiated nerves—wide-eyed and hesitant, the kind of new-in-town unease Ella recognized instantly.

Instinctively, she felt protective, suspicious of the boy. He seemed harmless enough—clean-shaven, wearing jeans, an oversized sweatshirt with a pickaxe logo, and a beanie, though it couldn't have been cooler than six-ty-five. Ella was about to put on her headphones to drown out the ambient buzz when something in the boy's story pulled her in.

"So get this," he started, leaning in just enough to make Ella do the same. "Back in the mid-1900s—like, literally around our age—this guy hits it big. Grandma gives him a graduation check, right? A couple hundred bucks or something, and instead of blowing it on a car or a trip, he throws it into the oil market. Hits the jackpot. Insane money.

So what does he do? Buys an entire mountain. Not a cabin. Not a plot. The *whole* damn mountain. Then he hires a crew from Peru—people no one local knew, no ties to the town—brings them in quietly, builds winding roads up through the trees. Nobody knew what was going on up there for years. Then he unveils it: his dream lodge. Fancy, remote, sitting at the peak like a crown. The locals thought it was weird, but rich people do weird stuff, right?

That's when people started disappearing. First it was only a few—teen hikers, a hunter who knew the woods like the back of his hand, a couple of kids from that little valley town at the base. Then it escalated. One of the missing? A student from here. Gone. Vanished. No bodies, no signs, no calls. Just... silence."

"Years passed. Then decades. People talked, rumors swirled, but the guy? Untouchable. Owned the land, paid his taxes, smiled for the papers. Meanwhile, the missing list kept growing. And you wanna know the sick part? When they finally caught him—late '70s—it was *by accident*. Some hikers stumbled on something near the lodge. Piles and piles of bones. Cops get called, warrants get signed, and what they found in that basement was straight nightmare fuel."

"He'd been *luring* them. Inviting some, tricking others. And once he had them? He played with them. Starved them until they were too weak to fight back, then beat them. Over and over. And when he was done? He dumped their bodies into a ravine behind the property. No markers. No graves. Just bones, scattered like trash.

The dude turned the whole mountain into his personal hunting ground. They said it took *years* to go through all the remains. Some of the skeletons? Still unidentified. No names. Just numbers in a box somewhere."

He leaned back, eyes glinting. "And the creepiest part? The lodge is still up there. Rotting in plain sight—being overtaken by nature. Empty. Or, you know... not."

"No way," a timid voice said beside him. The girl—maybe nineteen—sat on the edge of her chair, coffee clutched in both hands. She wore jean shorts and a yellow and black checkered flannel layered over a fitted tank top. Her brown hair was pulled back in a sleek ponytail. She couldn't have been much younger than Ella, but something in her wide-eyed stare made her look more innocent and naive. She listened like someone who was still trying to believe the world was safe.

"Thank goodness they caught him," she added, taking a slow sip of her drink.

"Well," the guy said, lowering his voice enough to make them all lean closer again, "that's the creepy part. Over the last couple years, people started going missing again."

The girl stiffened, hands tightening around the paper cup. "Is he still in jail?"

He paused, then grinned—not with joy, but with the slow curl of someone who *likes* a good scare. "No one knows," he said. "Apparently, there's no proof he ever existed to begin with."

Ella lurched forward.

She'd been trying, and failing, to pretend she wasn't listening, inching closer with every chilling detail. But *no proof?* That was insane. She was a trained investigative journalist. There's *always* proof. Somewhere. Someone saw something. Someone kept a record.

Losing her balance and her restraint, Ella turned her chair, inserted herself into their conversation, and said, louder than she meant to, "Of course there's proof!"

The two students turned toward her, confused, scowling in annoyance at the interruption.

"Where was this?" she pressed, undeterred. "I can find out. This is what I *do*."

"You hunt serial killers?" the girl asked, brow furrowed.

"What? No. I'm an investigative journalist," Ella said, straightening a bit, her voice laced with professional pride. Their shared look, somewhere between amusement and disbelief, burned a little. Like her title was a storybook role. Like they didn't get it.

"I can find out what happened to the guy," she said. "See if he was somehow released…"

"…Or escaped," the boy cut in, dropping his voice to a whisper, a playful smirk on his face.

The girl rolled her eyes and punched his shoulder lightly, but there was unease behind the gesture.

Ella didn't wait. She jumped up, crossed the space between them, and dropped into the empty chair at their table. Her journal thudded down in front of her, a pen already in hand. She flipped to a blank page.

"Tell me *everything* you know."

The students exchanged another glance, this one less amused, more guarded. The guy checked his watch.

"Look, uh... we need to get to class," he said quickly.

Without another word, they grabbed their bags, murmured something half-apologetic, and vanished into the crowd.

Ella sat frozen for a beat, staring at the empty page.

More questions than answers.

But that's what made it good.

She may be on leave, but she was still a journalist, and she knew a viral story when it landed in her lap.

Ella had a new quest.

CHAPTER FOUR

Mia Johnson

NOVEMBER, 2024

After another jarring pothole slammed her head against the window, Mia sat up, rubbing her temple as the family SUV bumped onto a gravel driveway. Outside, a figure was hunched over, furiously scrubbing at the otherwise new-looking sign that read *Welcome to Murdoch Manor*. The sound of their tires crunching over the stones made him jerk upright. He spun around fast, hiding his hands behind his back like a child caught red-handed.

But as the SUV rolled closer, it became clear, this wasn't a man. It was a teenage boy, lean and striking—his posture stiff and unsure—in front of the sign like a makeshift guard. His silky black hair veiled his eyes until he gave a quick puff, sending a few strands fluttering aside. A large bucket sat at his feet. His head was dipped slightly, his posture teetering between shame and defiance. Something about him looked...off. Like he'd been caught mid-act, though what exactly he was doing wasn't clear.

But as they drove by, his gaze lifted, and a slow, confident smile spread across his face. His teeth flashed white against his full, pink lips and mocha-toned skin, and Mia's heart skipped a beat. Boys rarely noticed her, but when he smiled at her, her insides melted. She glanced around the car, hoping no one had seen her goofy grin. But when her eyes landed on Rachel, her sister's eyes locked with the hot guy, Mia concluded with disappointment that maybe it wasn't her he'd been smiling at after all.

Mia had never given boys much thought—she found them immature for the most part and, frankly, smelly. But she could appreciate a good-looking guy when she saw one. Her sister, Rachel, on the other hand, was harder to read. Mia wasn't sure if Rachel noticed such things or was even interested in dating. She'd always seemed more invested in books and college plans than dating. But as Mia caught the faint blush spreading across Rachel's cheeks at the sight of the mysterious guy outside their window, she felt a pang of jealousy toward her sister for the first time in her life.

Not wanting to stare any longer, Mia forced her gaze forward as their car lumbered down the driveway. The family had originally booked a room at a grand hotel beside a historic mansion in Asheville, North Carolina, and Mia had been thrilled about touring the old house—famous for its nine regularly sighted ghosts. With her fascination with the supernatural and her supposed sixth sense, she'd been more excited than anyone. But *that* trip was scheduled for two weeks ago. When a complication at her mom's job resulted in a change of timing, so did their vacation. Mia was surprised the whole get-away hadn't been canceled.

Now, here they were in November, peak season in the North Carolina mountains, when the brilliant autumn colors drew in crowds from all over.

With every big-name hotel fully booked, her mom was thrilled to have found a newly-renovated mountain lodge that still had plenty of open rooms.

As the building loomed larger and they inched up the gravel driveway, a thrill ran through Mia's gut. This wasn't a fancy hotel or even a cozy cottage but an oversized, old cabin. Adding to the carpet surround of previously bold-colored leaves, now fading into decay, the lifeless color scheme of the house made the entire scene look like an old sepia-toned photograph. The peak, seasonal colors appeared to have already passed this particular mountain by.

The log cabin was a relic of another time, its weathered timbers speaking to decades of wear but also a stubborn defiance against the elements. The structure was sprawling, larger than the rustic cabins Mia had seen on the ride up the mountain. A deep wraparound porch framed by rough-hewn beams was adorned with an assortment of rocking chairs, their paint long since having peeled away.

The roof, its deep slate gray color hardly visible, now carried a patchwork of moss and lichen, blending it almost seamlessly into the surrounding forest. Large stone chimneys bookended the cabin, their mortar cracked, hinted at roaring fires within. The windows, dozens of them, were framed by thick shutters that had grown uneven over time. Some hung slightly askew, and their rusty hinges creaked mournfully in the wind.

The structural logs themselves bore the marks of time and weather—knots protruding like scars, their surfaces split and grayed by years of sun and rain. Despite this, they exuded a certain strength, their thickness promising warmth and protection. Between the logs, the chinking had grown uneven, patched here and there with fresh mortar that stood out against the worn wood like a shameful confession of repairs.

The gravel drive was surprisingly smooth under their tires, much better than the ill-maintained road up the mountain, and a burst of colorful mums lined the front porch, contrasting with the wild, overgrown vegetation creeping up around the building.

As the car rolled to a stop, Mia's breath caught in her throat as her eyes landed on an eerie figure in one of the second-story windows. The glass was tinged gray, but even through the grime, she could distinctly see a girl about her age, standing motionless and staring back at her with a cold, expressionless gaze.

"A human head remains conscious for around 20 seconds after being decapitated," Mia blurted out.

"Not now, Mia," her mom muttered impatiently, touching up her lipstick in the visor mirror.

"Okay, Lisa," Mia replied with a pout.

"And Mia, can you please call us Mom and Dad while we're here? People think it's strange when you use our first names." Her father, David, made the request with his usual edge of irritation. He hated the habit—thought it disrespectful, almost performative. Her mother, Lisa, said less about it, and when she did, it was always with more understanding than critique.

The habit had roots. When Mia was little, she'd gotten lost at a playground. She screamed "Mom" a dozen times—maybe more—drawing glances from every woman nearby, but none of them turned out to be hers. One desperate "Lisa," though, and her mother spun around instantly. From that day on, first names became a form of safety. A beacon.

But if Mia were honest now, she didn't do it out of survival anymore. She liked the reaction it got. The double-takes. The confusion. The silent question in people's eyes: *What kind of family is this?*

Everyone in the car turned their heads toward the lodge, where a small group was emerging from the front door, descending the porch steps, and forming a neat line at the bottom.

With a sudden snap, their mom flipped the visor up and mumbled, "Manor my ass."

Lisa twisted around to face the kids in the backseat. "Let's get out and meet the welcome committee." She pasted an artificial smile on her lips. "Be polite, use your manners," she added, taking a deep breath before looking squarely at Mia. "And no weird facts. Understood?"

Mia didn't nod or even react. She simply crossed her arms and wondered how long this group would stand waiting for her family to pile out of the car. As she reached to open her own door, she heard a deep voice from the other side. The cute boy from the sign had appeared at Rachel's door, holding it open with a charming smile as he extended his hand to help her out.

Feeling a pang of second-hand embarrassment over the cheesy gesture, Mia reluctantly scooted behind Tenner to exit from the open door. But as Tenner hopped out, he slammed the door behind him without a second glance, leaving her sitting in the back seat, unnoticed.

CHAPTER FIVE

Rachel Johnson

NOVEMBER, 2024

A soft tingle lingered on Rachel's arm long after the cute boy let go of her hand. She ducked her chin to her shoulder, trying to hide her face, which she knew was crimson. Her palms were damp with sweat, and she wiped them on the back of her jeans hoping no one noticed—slipping her hands into her pockets to play off her nerves. She attempted to look up.

"Rachel," her mom's voice broke through her thoughts, the expression on her face making it evident it wasn't the first time she'd called her name.

Rachel's gaze darted between her mom and the group of staff in front of them.

"You're red," her mom pointed out with a chuckle.

Rachel stepped back, self-conscious, only to stomp on Mia's foot as her sister emerged from the car. Losing her balance, Rachel rolled her ankle and dropped to the ground like a sack of potatoes. Mortified, she glanced down at her hand, realizing it was covered in something wet... and red—not sweat or blood, but paint. Out of the corner of her eye, she eyed a pair of work boots stepping toward her, but to her dismay, it was only her dad, blissfully oblivious to the situation, blocking the cute boy who had been also moving in to help. With a sigh, Rachel stared at the outstretched hands of the two males coming to her rescue, only to notice the boy's hands were also covered in red paint.

"Whoops, sorry," he said with a lopsided grin, holding out his paint-smeared hand to help her up. "Let me show you where you can wash that off."

A cheerful voice broke in, "Introductions first!"

Rachel's eyes took in the scene at last—standing with their backs to the lodge was the welcome committee—or rather, the manor's staff. At the center was a short Hispanic woman who appeared to be her parents' age. To her right were two teenage boys.

"Welcome to Murdoch Manor!" she said warmly. "I'm Valentina Miller, and these are my boys, Jon and Manny," she gestured beside her, "and you've already met Matthew." She motioned toward the paint-smeared boy beside Rachel. She pronounced his name "Ma-chew," which made Rachel smile—it was both sweet and unexpectedly charming.

Instead of glancing back at Matthew, Rachel focused on the others. It was clear that Matthew and Manny were Valentina's sons with their dark eyes, black eyelashes and thick black hair, similar to that of Valentina's, but Jon didn't appear to be related. While the other boys had café-au-lait skin, Jon was tall and built, with a pale complexion that made the constellation of freckles across his face and arms stand out like the toasted spots on a tortilla. His bright red hair was a wild, curly afro that seemed to have a life of its own, catching the light like a fiery halo. His sharp green eyes peeked out beneath the unruly locks, full of mischief and curiosity, giving him an air of youthful exuberance despite his large frame. It was possible, of course, that Valentina referred to the entire staff as "her boys."

"I'm Lisa Johnson, and this is my husband, David," Rachel's mom said with a warm smile, slipping an arm around her dad's waist. She seemed to be relaxed and comfortable in her mom jeans and striped sweater. There's someone in each family who typically makes introductions and steps up at restaurants to put their name on the wait list. In their family, it was mom. In the privacy of their own home, dad was the talkative one, peppering everyone with questions about their day, about their friends, and quizzing them on historic facts. But, put him in a public setting and he clams up, handing their mom the reins without complaint. Despite his introverted nature, Rachel's dad stood there with a smile, sporting his cargo pants and faded college sweatshirt. He could pretend with the best of them. Mom's gesture of wrapping a hand around his waist was less PDA and more to keep him from running away under the guise of unpacking the car at a glacial pace.

"This is my college-bound daughter, Rachel, my thrill-seeking son, Tenner, and Mia..." Her eyes lingered on Mia in warning, clad head to toe in black with a piercing stare to match. "Mia is our resident expert in bizarre and occasionally unsettling trivia."

Everyone stared at Mia when Valentina cut in, "And this is Mr. Theo Murdoch, the owner of Murdoch Manor."

Rachel struggled to suppress a squeak, and tried to play it off as a cough. She hadn't detected the towering man until now. It wasn't until he raised his hand in a shy wave that he differentiated himself from the porch support beam. He looked like a skeleton draped in bleached skin, standing close to seven feet tall and barely broader than a scarecrow.

"Welcome," he said in a voice so deep that Rachel felt the bass vibrate through her bones. "We're delighted to have you at our cozy mountain lodge."

Rachel sneaked a glance at her family, wondering if anyone else was disturbed by the appearance of the imposing man, but her mom, dad, and even Tenner and Mia looked unfazed, their faces set in polite smiles.

"Manny, Jon, please help with the Johnson family's bags," Valentina instructed with a wave of her hand. "Matthew, take this young lady to the kitchen and give her some oil to clean off the paint."

Matthew offered Rachel his elbow, and she threaded her clean arm through his, blushing as they walked up the porch steps and crossed the threshold, like a royal couple making their grand entrance at a ball.

Rachel tried to keep calm as she walked arm in arm with the gorgeous boy and somehow was able to relax when she heard Mia's voice behind her asking Valentina, "Did you know that horned toads can squirt blood out of their eyes?"

Chapter Six

Mia Johnson

November, 2024

Mia watched as Rachel was escorted into the lodge like an awkward, first-time debutante. She considered letting her sister know that the back of her jeans were smeared with red paint, but decided against it, smiling to herself as she wondered who would eventually point it out. With her parents chatting away, Mia's attention drifted to the two boys carrying the luggage. Both were watching her. The one with lighter skin gave her a knowing smile, as if they shared a secret—he'd spotted the paint too and like her, opted not to say anything. Mia's smile grew, but when she looked at the other boy, Manny, her amusement faded. He stared back at her, his eyes dark and rimmed with circles, his jaw clenched and eyes unblinking. It was possible that he had been taken aback by her statement about horned toads which also prompted a chastising glare from her mother. But it seemed more like he was trying to intimidate her or maybe he just had an unnerving intensity, neither of which bothered Mia.

Mia was a loner, not needing the company or acceptance of others. However, as all loners can attest, she often finds herself among other loners. They flock to the same dark corners in the library, the outskirts of the cafeteria and the farthest spot from crowds for the occasional assembly. Mia knew which were actual loners like herself and which ones were acting out or "going through a phase". She'd yet to meet someone else like her, however. She was different—drawn to the strange, the supernatural, facts that made most people uncomfortable.

Often finding herself among the misfits, she'd met plenty of creeps and more than her fair share of staredowns. She was immune to intimidation. If Manny was trying to get under her skin, it was laughable. Instead of saying something or challenging him back, she ignored him and followed her parents up the lodge steps. No need to make an enemy on the first day.

The lodge's owner, Mr. Murdoch was saying something to the group and while Mia tried to be attentive, she was distracted by his appearance and couldn't help staring at him. Dressed in dark slacks and a fitted black turtleneck, he looked like a walking anatomy model. His pale skin stretched tight over his face, his cheekbones so pronounced she half-expected them to slice through. She wasn't scared, but intrigued. She would give up her rare tooth collection to know his back story.

"A human tooth has 36 calories," Mia whispered to herself.

Without warning, Manny bumped her with a bag as he brushed past, barely acknowledging her. Jon, the lighter-skinned boy, shot her an apologetic glance before following Manny upstairs.

"I live in the village below," Mr. Murdoch said, his deep voice and rigid posture giving his wide smile an almost eerie, clown-like quality. "As the owner, I like to welcome our guests, but Valentina here keeps Murdoch

Manor running. Hiring her has been my best business decision yet." He gestured toward her with a nod, and Valentina, though visibly uneasy, forced an unnatural smile and nodded.

"The boys and I are here during the day to serve meals, clean your rooms, refresh linens, and help with anything you need," Valentina added, glancing at each guest as if it was her pleasure to be at their service.

"Does that mean we're all alone at night?" Tenner asked, his voice filled with nervous excitement. His leg was shaking and his eyes searching over every visible surface. He was doing his best to heed his mother's instructions to be polite and behave, but was far from holding himself together. Mia could imagine the mischief he was already planning. Tenner was imaginative and creative to a fault. He could make any object, whether a piece of furniture or gnarled tree, into a dangerous challenge.

Lisa shot him a scolding look but also glanced at Valentina with curiosity as if willing her to answer her son's question.

Valentina laughed. "Not at all. My boys take turns staying overnight. They have a bed in the office right behind the front desk." She pointed to a closed door behind a large, rustic wooden counter that looked as if it were carved directly from a tree. The knots and natural curves accented the front, while the top was smooth, holding an old-fashioned bell and a large reservation book—no computer or phone in sight. Mia assumed there must be some kind of tech hidden somewhere. No modern lodge could run without an online reservation system, right?

"If you need anything, one of us will always be nearby," Valentina assured them with a kind smile.

"You're in good hands with Valentina and her boys," Mr. Murdoch said, stepping around the group and out the door. "I hope you enjoy your stay, and I'll see you again on a future visit!"

Mia and Tenner watched, in amazement, as he approached a rusty-red, two-door coupe, wondering how he'd fit his giant frame into the small car. But with surprising ease, he slid inside, closed the door, and drove down the gravel road. As the sound of the car tires crunching over the rocks faded, Valentina seemed to relax, letting out a deep breath before flashing a genuine smile. "Now, allow me to show you around."

CHAPTER SEVEN

Rachel Johnson

NOVEMBER, 2024

With each step, Rachel felt her walk with Matthew grow more awkward. Though he wasn't as imposing as Mr. Murdoch, Matthew still towered over her five-foot-four frame, making her feel less like she was being escorted and more like she was being towed along, hanging from his elbow. His support should have been helpful with her throbbing ankle, but as much as she enjoyed the touch of his arm against hers, she couldn't wait to pull away. When he placed his other hand over her arm, as if to steady her further, her stomach lurched.

Needing an excuse to break contact, Rachel slipped her arm free and crouched to retie her shoe, willing away the nausea as she fumbled with the laces. Sweat beaded on her forehead, and all she wanted was to pull off her itchy sweater, but the thought of lifting it over her head, even with a tank top beneath, felt way too risque. Her damp palms smeared the red paint on her hand, streaking it onto her shoelaces. Finally, she got the shoe tied and rose slowly, wiping her brow and taking a steadying breath.

"So," she said, forcing herself to look at Matthew while pointedly keeping her hands to herself. "You were painting the sign?" She cringed at her own question—she'd seen him at the sign and he was clearly covered in red paint. How had she not noticed that when he helped her out of the car?

"Not exactly," Matthew chuckled, running a hand across his forehead, flashing a casual yet charming smile. Rachel looked away, trying to keep her cool as she waited for him to continue.

"I was trying to remove paint from the sign. Some local kids vandalized it," he said, leading her through the lodge's great room toward the kitchen.

Curious by nature, Rachel wanted to linger and absorb the room's details, but she kept her eyes fixed on him. "Someone vandalized it? Way up here? What did they do?"

"They changed 'Murdoch Manor' to 'Murder Manor,'" he said with a laugh.

Rachel stopped, her smile fading despite his light tone. "Why would they do that?" she asked, her curiosity tinged with concern. People didn't alter signs to say "Murder" without some reason behind it. Had something bad happened here?

Matthew's gaze dropped, and he shifted uneasily. "Some local kids being kids, I guess," he replied, his tone less carefree now. A strange thing to say as he was little more than a kid himself.

Without looking back, he pushed the swinging kitchen door, holding it open for Rachel to enter. Normally, if someone dangled a mystery in front of her like that, she would dig for details until she had answers. But with Matthew, her usual confidence felt deflated and her tongue tangled. So, for now, she kept her questions to herself and followed him into the kitchen.

Matthew let the door swing shut behind him and moved around to where Rachel stood. The kitchen looked exactly how she'd imagined a mountain lodge kitchen would: rustic and homey, with a mix of old and new. The appliances gleamed like they'd been recently updated, but the dated cabinets and well-worn woodblock countertops hinted at years of use. A deep farmhouse sink sat empty with a neat stack of drying dishes to one side. Next to a small soap dispenser, a bud vase held a sprig of holly complete with tiny red berries, reminding her it was wintertime, even though snow had yet to blanket the mountains. A large rolling island dominated the room, its surface dusted in flour with two mounds of dough resting under tea towels. Shelves lined the walls, stacked with cookbooks, mismatched country towels, and jars of cooking supplies. Rachel could imagine Valentina whipping up meals with ease, adding to the warm atmosphere. Yet, as a draft brushed the back of her neck, a strange unease settled in her chest.

Matthew crossed the room, pulling a bottle of olive oil from a high shelf. "Mom says this'll help get the paint off," he said, blushing slightly. "Sorry again about that."

Rachel walked to the sink, letting the water heat up before pouring oil into her hands and rubbing them together. The paint started to lift immediately, so she added a squirt of soap, scrubbing until the greasy residue faded. She glanced around, looking for a clean towel, but before she could search further, Matthew held a faded checkered towel out to her.

She took it and dried her hands, only to feel his gaze linger. She looked up and saw him staring at a spot right above her eyes.

"You've got a bit on your forehead," he said, as she turned back to the sink in shame, wiping at the spot. "And... on the back of your pants."

Rachel clenched her teeth, fighting the urge to scream. Not only had she been walking around with paint on her hand, but she had managed to smear the paint on both her pants and face. Embarrassment stung, and tears pricked at her eyes. What felt like a sweet romantic moment filled with budding sexual tension a moment ago now made her want to run down the mountain, never to return.

This wasn't like her. She was emotional and her feelings were unfamiliar. She was focused on college, her career, and building a successful life. Relationships and crushes were low on her list, something for "later." But, as she stood at the sink on the verge of tears, she knew that for the first time, someone had lit the fire she had fought to keep extinguished until she was ready.

Matthew was kind and gorgeous, so she'd allowed herself to feel something— only to end up here, covered in paint and feeling completely ridiculous.

CHAPTER EIGHT

Mia Johnson

NOVEMBER, 2024

Mia lingered at the back as the group drifted into the great room. Her mom was following Valentina with a pep in her step, hanging on her every word, a death grip on her dad's arm, dragging him behind. Mia took it upon herself to keep an eye on Tenner. She knew that if left to his own devices, he'd be back outside, racing through the woods and getting lost in no time.

The room had the cozy, loft aesthetic of an A-frame cabin, with high ceilings and a stone fireplace that stretched all the way up the wall. Though unlit, the fireplace was neatly stacked with logs. Unmatching, plush sofas and armchairs that looked like they'd been thrifted or picked up at a yard sale, filled the space. Seating was interspersed with end tables crafted from the same rustic wood as the counter in the foyer. Each chair was draped with a fluffy blanket, inviting guests to settle in. Candles adorned most of the tables, alongside coffee table books featuring mountain landscapes. To the left, large windows framed the view of the front porch, while to the right, a large banquet table stretched the length of the wall. Mia wondered if all the wooden furniture was made from local trees. She craned her neck to look up at the wall above the table to spot a long balcony overlooking the great room—likely a mezzanine leading to the guest rooms.

A door in the far corner of the room opened, giving a fleeting view of the kitchen as Rachel and Matthew emerged to join the group.

"Oh, good, all cleaned up," Valentina said with a smile aimed at Rachel, before casting a disapproving glance at Matthew. "You should do the same," she added sternly.

With a shrug, Matthew extended his hand, and Valentina dropped a set of keys into it. "See you back at home," she said warmly, her expression softening as she smiled at him.

Matthew turned to leave, but not without stealing a quick look back at Rachel. Mia couldn't help but find it amusing to watch her older sister flustered like this. Rachel, who was usually all about self-reliance, independence, and keeping her cool, was suddenly weak-kneed over a boy she barely knew. It was a rare—and telling—glimpse into a side of Rachel she hadn't seen before.

"I'm sure you'd all like to get settled. Manny will show you to your rooms while Jon and I start on dinner," Valentina announced with a warm smile.

Rachel turned toward the stairs, only to come face-to-face with Manny, who had appeared silently at her side. She yelped, clutching her chest in surprise. Her parents chuckled awkwardly, equally startled by the solemn boy's sudden presence. Mia smirked in approval. Manny briefly caught her eye but didn't offer a word or even a hint of a smile. Instead, he simply turned and headed up the stairs, not bothering to see if anyone was following.

As Mia followed her parents and Rachel back toward the foyer, she realized that Tenner was missing. She quickly scanned the room: the others crossed back into the foyer, Manny was already halfway up the stairs, but there was no sign of Tenner. Had he slipped into the kitchen for a snack? Maybe he'd sneaked outside when Matthew left?

Mia turned, searching for clues. No lumps under the blankets on the couch, no shoes poking out from under the tables. The kitchen door had stopped swinging, and the logs in the fireplace looked undisturbed—at first. Then her gaze landed on the fireplace again, and she watched as a small rock tumbled down from the stone surround to the hearth.

Mia's eyes widened as she looked up to see Tenner clinging to the tall stone fireplace like a rock wall, at least fifteen feet off the ground.

"Tenner," she hissed angrily, trying to keep her voice down. "Tenner!" she repeated, a bit louder.

Tenner looked over his shoulder at her, grinning. "Cool, huh?"

"Get down before they see you," Mia snapped through clenched teeth, shooting him a warning look.

Tenner sighed dramatically, then began his descent. "Party pooper," he muttered under his breath as his feet hit the ground.

CHAPTER NINE

Maryanne Maxwell

MAY, 1954

Maryanne Maxwell struggled to stay conscious. Her head throbbed with a relentless, stabbing pain as she lay on her back, feeling her hair sticky with blood against the cold floor. Squinting against the blinding light pouring through the windows, she found herself staring up at the towering stone fireplace. She tried to piece together how she'd ended up there, but her mind was a haze. Had she hit her head by accident? Had she tripped on a loose stone?

The last clear memory was of her getting ready at home. She'd spent hours primping, making herself appear older and more professional than her eighteen years. Her light brown hair had been carefully twisted into a chignon and secured with a pearl comb she'd borrowed from her mother's jewelry box. Not a single strand out of place.

Today was supposed to be the most important day of her life. She dreamed of going to college, of pushing against every barrier set by a society that saw women like her as little more than homemakers. She was driven and ambitious, inspired by the rare women who had broken ground in law and justice. Her parents, however, couldn't have disagreed more—they didn't believe a "proper woman" needed an education beyond home economics and childcare, and they'd refused to support her dreams.

Maryanne wanted more. She dreamed of graduating at the top of her university class, of going to law school, of arguing cases in high-profile courtrooms. But first, she needed money. Desperation had led her to secretly read through the help wanted ads in the Sunday newspaper, where she found an opportunity that felt like fate—a reception position at a new hotel. Like every high school girl, she'd taken typing and hospitality classes—she could handle the front desk and even clean rooms if necessary. Though the hotel was over an hour away, the job included room and board. It would allow her to finally leave home, earn her keep, and begin working toward her future. She didn't need anyone else to believe in her dreams. She believed in herself and that was all she needed.

Determined, she'd spent the last of her saved allowance on a professional dress for the interview and resolved to go it alone. She hadn't wanted her parents to know, fearing they'd stop her.

Now, as her blurry gaze drifted down the stone fireplace and caught sight of her once—pristine polyester dress, she felt a wave of regret. She wished she hadn't been so brave, that she'd confided in someone about where she was going. Her memories returned in sharp fragments, and the truth flooded her mind. She hadn't hit her head by accident. She hadn't tripped on a loose stone.

She'd been murdered.

Chapter Ten

Rachel Johnson

November, 2024

The sinking feeling of disappointment Rachel felt when Matthew walked out was short-lived, ending abruptly with the shock of coming face-to-face with his brother, Manny. The guy was odd. There was no other way to put it. He had dark, emotionless eyes, pools of void that seemed to hold no trace of humanity, as if they absorbed rather than reflected light. His face was an unchanging mask of indifference, with no trace of smiles, frowns, or any hint of sentiment. His expression was so devoid of life that it seemed carved from stone, a visage that made Rachel question whether he was a mere observer—or something far more dangerous. Her heart raced and her sweaty palms threatened to return. As she followed behind him, up the stairs to the second floor, she couldn't shake the fear that he would turn around and look at her.

When they reached the landing, Rachel ducked behind her parents, her shoulder colliding with Tenner as he raced past. Mia trailed behind yelling, "One hundred billion people have died in human history."

The second floor opened into a long hallway, open on one side as a balcony overlooking the great room below. On the other side were four heavy wooden doors, their knobs old and tarnished, flanked by two more doors at the ends—one near the stairs and another at the opposite end of the hall. The dark green fabric wallpaper clung to the walls like a relic of a bygone era, fraying at the edges. If this was "newly renovated," Rachel thought, Mr. Murdoch must have been aiming for a haunted museum vibe.

Manny stepped aside, his silent gesture directing them toward the suitcases set neatly outside each door. Without waiting for acknowledgement, he turned and stalked back down the creaking stairs, his absence leaving the group letting out a collective exhale.

Rachel's mother gawked as the so-called help vanished into the great room. "Well," she said, recovering quickly, "it looks like we're taking whichever rooms our bags are in front of." She pointed them out one by one: "Rachel, you're here, first on the right. Mia, next door. Tenner, this one's yours. And your dad and I have the last one."

Smiling at them all, she added, "Get settled and cleaned up. Let's meet downstairs in an hour."

Rachel moved toward her door but stopped when Mia's voice broke through. "What's that door?" She was pointing to a smaller, nondescript door between her and Tenner's rooms.

Their mother stepped over and opened it without pause to reveal a surprisingly modern bathroom. Sparkling white tiles gleamed under the lights, and polished chrome fixtures adorned the double sinks. Fluffy white towels were stacked neatly on racks and in baskets, and the bathtub-shower combination looked brand new. The contrast to the rest of the house was jarring.

With a nod, their mother turned away. Tenner, however, had other ideas. He sped past her and made for the unclaimed door at the end of the hall, his hand on the knob before anyone could stop him.

"Tenner, don't! What if someone's staying there?" Rachel scolded, her face flushing with panic.

He twisted the knob a few times, but it wouldn't budge. Giving up with a huff, he retreated to his own room, slamming the door behind him.

Rachel sighed, her tension finally easing, and opened the door to her room.

CHAPTER ELEVEN

Mia Johnson

NOVEMBER, 2024

Mia leaned her back against the closed door of her assigned room, relieved to escape the hallway drama. Rachel had been acting uncharacteristically frazzled, and Tenner seemed determined to stir up chaos. Honestly, if he had fallen off that enormous fireplace and broken his neck, it would have put a serious damper on their vacation. Pulling her phone from the deep pocket of her oversized black hoodie, she typed, "deaths by fireplace falls." The signal was horrible allowing for only the text to load with broken images and even that took forever. The results were predictably dominated by Christmas Eve mishaps, and with a sigh, she pocketed her phone.

She took a moment to survey the room. The decor reminded her of the Colonial Williamsburg tour her elementary school had taken years ago—stuffy and dated. The smell was a layered, complex aroma that carried mildew along with the weight of time, filling Mia's nose with a faint mustiness, like air that hasn't moved freely in decades. The scent of old wood dominated, a warm, earthy fragrance tinged with the faint sharpness of varnish long faded.

Twin beds, their frames scuffed and chipping, lined the narrow room, with an antique nightstand between them. A tall, skinny window at the far end overlooked the back of the lodge, which perched along the side of a mountain. The forest beyond stretched endlessly, a stark mix of leafless branches and scattered evergreens. Even in the fading twilight, she could make out the beginning of a trail winding into the trees. Maybe she could convince Tenner to explore it with her—if he wasn't too busy trying to get himself killed.

"Many deaths-by-fall are intentional," Mia said to the empty room.

She sat on the edge of one of the beds, running her fingers across the stiff, scratchy bedspread. It felt like it had been starched within an inch of its life. Shifting her weight experimentally, she winced as the mattress springs creaked ominously, threatening to burst through the fabric. Deciding she wasn't in the mood to "get settled" or "clean up" as instructed, she opted to snoop around instead.

The nightstand drawer yielded nothing, not even the standard-issue Bible. Dropping to her knees, she peered under the beds, finding only thick layers of dust that made her wrinkle her nose to fight off a sneeze. She briefly considered calling Manny to clean it up but thought better of it—staying on his good side seemed like a survival tactic at this point.

As she pushed herself up, her eyes caught something unusual in the floorboards under one of the beds. The pattern was off. As the bed frames were too low for her to crawl under, she shoved her shoulder against the base and stretched her arm beneath as far as it would go. Her fingers brushed over a section of wood that felt ever so slightly raised, and then—a metal latch.

CHAPTER TWELVE

Ella Whitmore

OCTOBER, 2024

Ella had spent the better part of a week combing through internet forums, old newspaper archives, and local libraries—even borrowing her friend's student ID to slip into the university library—searching for any mention of a so-called *serial killer hotel* tucked somewhere in the North Carolina mountains. But no matter how deep she dug, she came up empty.

Sure, it was entirely possible the story was nothing more than campus folklore—urban legend repackaged to spook freshmen. But something about it tugged at her. A detail she couldn't quite name. A weight behind the words. It didn't feel like just a story.

Unwilling to let it go, Ella shifted tactics. She began scouring business licenses and property records. The mountain range stretched endlessly, but she narrowed her search to a thirty-mile radius around the university, planning to spiral outward from there.

To her surprise, the research moved fast. Registered hotels, lodges, bed-and-breakfasts—all easy to track, most just as easy to eliminate. Chains were ruled out instantly. Others didn't match the timeline.

She was lucky, in a way. The era of strangers casually renting out their homes to travelers hadn't quite taken hold during the time the murders supposedly occurred. That particular headache—untraceable Airbnbs and forgotten listings—was one she could avoid.

Within days Ella had been able to eliminate all lodging establishments within thirty miles and expanded her search to sixty. It was there she got her first hit. A boutique hotel by the name of French Broad (named after the river running through the town, much to her disappointment), located in Hot Springs, North Carolina was roughly 50 miles from Boone. Established in the 70's, the quaint hotel became a mountain destination for winter and summer travelers alike. It wasn't until the 90's when a chain erected their new, 'economy' motel next door, that the business took a hit. They closed not long after. It was close but the timeline didn't quite fit if the would-be serial killer was sent to jail in the 70s. But that's assuming the kid at the coffee shop knew the correct dates.

The second hit was hardly a hotel, more of a mountain lodge. The Hilltop Escape sat atop a small mountain looming above the quaint town of Maple Ridge, North Carolina. The only information she found on the place was the opening of the business in 1952 and their closing in 1975. On the 28th page of her search results for "Hilltop Escape, Maple Ridge, NC" Ella found construction plans, which detailed a log-cabin like design with five bedrooms and a commercial kitchen. She imagined it being a place for corporate retreats or family reunions, not big enough to book hundreds of travelers a night like an actual hotel. The name on the property records was Elias Thornfield.

Ella found no information about the lodge, mountain, or owner after 1975. She had no clue whether it had been rebranded, demolished, or left to rot beneath the trees. The address itself appeared to be non-existent. Even a map search of the location came back as invalid.

She'd found as much as she could remotely. Her only option moving forward was to visit Maple Ridge.

CHAPTER THIRTEEN

Rachel Johnson

NOVEMBER, 2024

Rachel let out a disgusted groan as she unzipped her suitcase, taking in the details of the room. They could've been vacationing at a five-star resort in Asheville.

But here they were in the supposed *renovated* mountain lodge. With the exception of the bathroom and kitchen appliances, Rachel seriously doubted anything had been updated in nearly three-quarters of a century. In her opinion, they would all have been happier staying home when they had to cancel the original trip. Rachel had college plans to make. Sure, she was only a Junior but it was essential that she keep her perfect GPA. She had volunteer hours to earn, and don't even get her started on her college essay. Tenner would have no doubt preferred spending his break hanging out with friends. And Mia... well, who knew what Mia liked to do but certainly she'd rather be doing whatever she does holed up in that dark room of hers. Yet here they were, in an ancient lodge in the middle of nowhere.

Her room was small, as most mid-twentieth-century rooms were. The bed was barely large enough to qualify as a double, its wooden frame scratched by time and use. The nightstand, narrow and worn, stood next to a small window that overlooked the back of the lodge, its view framed by the deepening twilight. An antique desk sat in the corner, its polished surface reflecting the dim light of the dusty overhead fixture. The room was quaint, she supposed, but there was something about it—the way the walls seemed to press in a little too tightly—that made Rachel feel the pressing need to open the door.

She set to unpacking, pulling her clothes from the suitcase and laying them neatly into the stiff drawers of the dresser. Each drawer groaned in protest, their faded floral liners releasing a faint musty scent. She wrinkled her nose but continued folding and arranging her clothes with care. Once her suitcase was empty, she turned to the desk, placing her supplies with deliberate precision: a no-nonsense notebook with crisp, lined pages, her slim laptop, a rainbow of pens, and several rolls of cheerful washi tape. She smiled faintly as she surveyed the arrangement. It was a small touch of order, a sense of control in the chaos of an unfamiliar house. Later, she'd settle in to brainstorm ideas for her college essay.

Satisfied, Rachel moved to the side of the bed and sat on the edge. She leaned back on her hands, exhaling deeply, but the moment of relief was short-lived. A chill ran up her spine, making her shiver. She straightened and glanced at the window. It was shut tight, its glass panes slightly fogged from the evening air. Her eyes scanned the room for a vent or some other source of the draft, but the walls were bare, and the stillness of the room remained unbroken.

The chill lingered, gnawing at the edges of her nerves. She stood, wrapping her arms around herself, and glanced at the far side of the bed, where the corner of the room seemed more sheltered. Without allowing herself time to dwell on the odd unease, she grabbed her pillow and moved to the other side of the bed, tucking herself against the wall. Pulling the blanket over her legs, she willed herself to relax.

"Just tired," she murmured, her voice barely audible. But her eyes flew back to the indentation she'd left where she'd been sitting. The faint outline of her presence seemed to hold, like a shadow refusing to fade, and she half-expected something—or someone—to appear.

Shaking her head, she stood again, grabbing her cube-shaped bag of toiletries. Maybe a hot shower would help chase away the eerie sensation, but as she left the room, the chill still clung to her, like an unwelcome guest she couldn't quite shake.

Chapter Fourteen

Mia Johnson

November, 2024

The wood was rough and worn beneath Mia's fingers, and the metal latch felt cool to the touch. She strained to slide a finger through the ring of the latch, finally managing to lift it. The lid opened with surprising ease, but it quickly became clear that the wooden door was too large to fully open under the low bed frame. Careful not to let it slam shut on her fingers, Mia guided the lid against her wrist, holding it steady as she slipped her hand into the hidden compartment.

The space beneath the floorboards was shallow, the base a few inches below the opening. Though her shoulder and arm ached from the awkward stretch, it only took moments for her hand to explore the space. Her fingers brushed against nothing but the smooth, wooden sides. Disappointed, she withdrew her arm, letting the lid fall back into place with a thud.

Mia sat back on her knees, rolling her shoulders to ease the tension, and let out a slow breath. If her room had a hidden compartment, there was a good chance the lodge held more secrets. The idea tugged at her curiosity, and she decided to head downstairs.

From the top of the stairs, Mia noted her mom was already in the great room below. She was talking animatedly with someone out of sight, her gestures sharp and deliberate. Whatever the conversation was about, it was intense enough that even the creaky stairs didn't pull her attention.

Mia padded down quietly and slipped into an oversized chair, pulling a blanket over her legs. From her new angle, she could see the hostess, Valentina, seated on the couch opposite her mom. The two women were so deeply engrossed in their discussion that neither appeared to even notice Mia's arrival. She settled deep into the chair, intrigued, straining to catch fragments of their conversation while the blanket's warmth enveloped her.

"I'm the breadwinner," Lisa said proudly, her voice a touch too bright, while Mia shifted in her seat, cringing at the thinly veiled brag. "I'm a project manager for a software company. Our vacation plans revolve around my software releases. If it doesn't launch, neither do we," she added with a laugh. "That's how we ended up here instead of a luxurious spa in Asheville."

Then, as if suddenly aware of how sharp that sounded, she softened. "But hey—look how great this turned out. Everything happens for a reason, right?"

Valentina cleared her throat gently and steered the conversation elsewhere, asking about David.

"He works part-time as a substitute teacher," Lisa explained to Valentina, her tone carrying a faint trace of embarrassment that only Mia would notice. It was a subtle shift, one Mia had come to recognize—a delicate attempt to justify her husband's situation. "He had a pretty severe brain injury during his final year of college football." Her mother's voice softened, growing almost wistful as she fell into her familiar narrative. Mia could practically recite it by heart, down to the pauses and inflections.

"You should have seen him in his prime," Lisa continued. "He was all-conference every year and even a Heisman candidate. Then, in one game, an illegal tackle ended it all—his career, his dreams of going pro. It was devastating."

Valentina responded with a sympathetic *tutt-tutt* as Lisa pressed on. "He recovered after years of grueling physical therapy and managed to finish his degree online. But the migraines..." Lisa shook her head. "They're still so debilitating. He can't hold down a full-time job, but thankfully, my work is enough to support the family."

Her tone brightened, the well-rehearsed silver lining slipping into place. "Honestly, it's been a blessing in disguise. He was able to stay home with the kids when they were younger and now he's around when they get home from school."

Mia smirked, already predicting what her mom would say next. *And he's become a fabulous cook,* she thought, as Lisa added, "Not to mention he's become a fabulous cook."

Finally, her mother seemed to exhaust the speech, seamlessly pivoting. "Anyway, what does your husband do?"

The awkward pause that preceded Valentina's answer brought the atmosphere in the room from sad to downright depressing.

Chapter Fifteen

Annette Engberg

July, 1959

With 5 years of marital bliss, her 23 year marriage was over. Annette Engberg wanted a divorce the second their youngest son moved out of the house, but that would've been foolish. The highest achievement she could list on a resume was her high school diploma, and that wasn't worth the paper on which it was printed. She had no money of her own and having never held a job, she had no idea how she could support herself.

Marrying her high school sweetheart seemed like the right move at the time. In fact, with Joe moving from Seattle to the east coast for college, it was the only way they could stay together. Her parents would've locked her up and thrown away the key had she tried to run off with a boy. Four short months after their wedding and cross country move to central North Carolina, Annette was pregnant with their first son. Five years later, Joe had a shiny new job and Annette had 3 kids under 4 years old. In addition to the strain of raising three young boys, she kept the house clean, the yard well-maintained, and warm meals on the table. Joe rose the corporate ladder with a quickness that was only rivaled by his spike in confidence. With his rapid success came more money, a bigger home, and a personal secretary.

The man who enjoyed showing off his wife, his home, his growing boys, eventually turned into a man who rarely graced them with his presence. While Joe was kept warm in the beds of his ever changing secretaries, he still provided Annette and her kids with a good life. They lived in a beautiful, gated neighborhood, the boys went to the best schools, and, as they grew up and needed less of her, she spent more time at the country club where she would play golf, lunch with friends, and unwind under the strong hands (and body) of her masseuse.

It wasn't long before Annette's feelings for Joe morphed from love to indifference. Maybe had she left him when she was younger she would've been able to remarry into the same lifestyle, but that was not a chance she was prepared to take. Divorce was becoming common, but if the woman left—more times than not—she left empty-handed.

The jobs that Annette was qualified for would never afford her to live the life she was accustomed to, so she played the long game portraying the perfect housewife and mother. Her hard work and patience paid off when he could no longer get it up, putting an end to his extra marital affairs and more importantly, her wifely duties.

After marrying off their youngest son, Annette began adding small amounts of rat poison to Joe's morning coffee. It only took three days of gradually increasing the dosage for Joe to begin to show flu-like symptoms. But Joe being Joe refused to see a doctor. Annette even encouraged him to get checked if only to enjoy his stubborn refusal. By day five his hair started falling out in clumps and the vomiting began. He never woke up for day six.

Her only regret was the grief her sons' would have to endure, but all three of them were happily married and one with a child on the way. They would get over it. Her sweet boys stayed a couple days after the funeral to help Annette go through Joe's things. They took what they wanted and boxed up the rest to go into storage. When they left, she called the local donation center to pick up the boxes. She wasn't wasting any money on storage.

The house was too big for her when Joe was alive. She was tired of cleaning the monstrosity. After an expected bereavement period, she listed the house for sale. To make showings easy on her agent, Annette took off to the mountains for a vacation.

The outside of the lodge where she was staying was rustic, but the bathroom next to her room looked like it came out of a magazine. The sink, toilet, and bath were all avocado green, the hottest new color trend. Mustard colored shag rugs lined the floors and toilet seat. She would have to remember that avocado green for her next bathroom design.

The only thing the bathroom seemed to be missing was a functional door lock. As she was currently the only lodger, it hadn't seemed like it would be a problem. The steady hum of the overhead fan provided the perfect therapeutic atmosphere as she lowered herself into the hot water and bubbles.

If only she'd thought to block the door. Or maybe, if she'd gotten out of the tub when she started to get sleepy. When she suddenly awoke, it wasn't water in her lungs that kept her from breathing but the hands that held her under squeezing her neck like a vice. She couldn't see her attacker through the bubbles, but could feel the strong hands. No kicking or flailing could loosen the grip that was getting tighter by the second. A loud pop echoed through her ears and she lost all feeling in her body as the figure backed away and allowed her to float to the top. She couldn't move, she couldn't breathe, and she couldn't even blink, but for her last precious seconds of life she could still see that magnificent avocado green.

Chapter Sixteen

Rachel Johnson

November, 2024

The bathroom was quiet, save for the steady hum of the overhead fan and the soft patter of water droplets hitting the tub as Rachel adjusted the shower temperature. She'd locked the door, double-checked it even, but as the steam began to fill the room, a heavy foreboding settled over her. It was ridiculous, she told herself. This was an unfamiliar house. Still, her gaze lingered on the shower curtain as she stepped into the tub, pulling it closed with a faint scrape of the rings against the metal rod.

The hot water poured over her, soothing away the tension in her shoulders. For a moment, she allowed herself to relax, letting the warmth cascade over her skin. But as she lathered shampoo into her hair, the feeling of panic returned. It teased at the back of her neck, a gnawing sensation that someone—or something—was on the other side of the curtain. She froze mid-scrub, listening. The faint creak of the house settling echoed somewhere distant, but nothing else.

"Get a grip, Rachel," she muttered under her breath, shaking her head as she worked the shampoo deeper into her hair.

With her eyes closed to rinse the suds, the sensation of watchful eyes heightened. Her heart thudded against her ribs. *Was that a shadow shifting behind the curtain?* She fought the urge to look, forcing herself to stay still. The water streaming down her face masked everything, but suddenly, she felt it—something crawling up her arm.

Rachel's eyes flew open as she let out a strangled gasp, blindly slapping at her arm. Her fingers fumbled through the suds as she frantically washed the shampoo from her eyes, blinking away the sting. Her vision cleared, and there it was—a tangled clump of her own hair, freed from her scalp and plastered to her skin.

She exhaled a shaky laugh, her hands trembling as she peeled the hair away and flung it toward the drain. "You're losing it," she whispered to herself, turning off the water and stepping out of the shower.

Wrapping a towel around herself, Rachel stood before the fogged-up mirror. She reached for the hair dryer but froze mid-motion. Something about the mirror caught her eye—a faint, foggy outline that seemed to shift as she moved. Her breath hitched as her mind conjured up all sorts of terrifying possibilities.

Nope. She wasn't doing this. Tossing the hairdryer back onto the counter, she secured the towel around her and backed out of the bathroom. Air drying sounded fine. Anything to escape that suffocating room.

Chapter Seventeen

Mia Johnson

November, 2024

"**M**y husband, Will, passed away three years and six months ago," Valentina began, her voice steady but tinged with sadness. She chuckled awkwardly, adding, "Not that I'm keeping track."

Mia, curled up tighter under the blanket, half-listening, her eyes heavy from the warmth of the crackling fire. Across the room, her mom leaned forward, her expression soft and sympathetic as Valentina continued.

"Will and I moved here when the kids were still in grade school. He was working for a startup company that was developing a new app, and when they relocated their headquarters, we followed. The owner found an old building here—'a real steal', apparently, and perfect for their ambitious growth plans. For a while, everything was great. The kids settled in quickly, and I loved being home with them. But then..." Valentina paused, her voice lowering, "one by one, employees began getting sick."

Lisa gasped audibly, jolting Mia fully awake.

Valentina pressed on. "It wasn't until the first death and several severe illnesses that they re-inspected the building and discovered it was riddled with asbestos."

Lisa, ever the problem-solver, jumped in. "How could something like that happen? Surely someone was held accountable?" She caught herself and softened her tone. "Did your husband—did Will...?"

Mia caught movement out of the corner of her eye and turned her head, her heart racing at the sudden appearance. The banquet table sat empty, the kitchen door remained closed. No one was there. Mia quickly looked back in surprise to the only other people in the room, Valentina and her mom.

Valentina nodded, her gaze dropping to her lap. "Aggressive Pleural Mesothelioma. The massive short-term exposure combined with constant airflow past the contamination was an invisible danger no one saw coming. Will and all five of his coworkers were eventually diagnosed. They all... passed away."

Mia's heart sank at the solemnity of Valentina's tone. She brushed off her feeling of unease and sank back into the chair, allowing her eyes to grow heavy again watching the dancing flames in the fireplace. She heard the shuffling of fabric and imagined Valentina crossing herself and bowing her head in prayer. Mia was eager for the chef to continue as her voice was soothing and melodic, as though she were telling a lullaby rather than recounting a tragedy.

Indoor air can be two to five times more polluted than outdoor air, Mia thought to herself.

"Most of the newer employees worked in another part of the building," Valentina continued. "Maybe it was luck, or maybe the shorter exposure saved them. But yes, someone was held liable. The state found that an inspector had been falsifying reports—not out of malice, just sheer laziness and negligence. They awarded sizable settlements to the families."

Lisa hesitated, noting the almost embarrassed look on Valentina's face at the word *sizable* before asking what Mia had been wondering too. "Then why... why are you working here?"

Valentina's gaze swept the room, lingering on the exposed beams and crackling fire. "This place... this damn place," she muttered, catching herself with an apologetic glance at Mia. "Sorry, dear."

With a nod from both Lisa and Mia, she continued. "This was supposed to be mine. When we moved to town, the lodge was abandoned, owned by a woman suffering from dementia. With no living relatives, it sat empty. When she passed, Will and I tried to buy it, but we were turned down for a loan. Then, weeks later, Will fell ill. Everything spiraled after that."

Valentina sighed deeply, smoothing her apron neatly on her lap. "On his deathbed, Will finalized the settlement and begged me to follow my dream of opening a bed and breakfast. I promised him I would, though it was the last thing I cared about at the time. But eventually, it gave me something to focus on, something other than my grief."

Her voice grew more animated. "The lodge sat in probate for six months while they searched for heirs. No one had even inquired about the property the previous fifty years. It was mine for the taking. I prepared a business plan, lined up contractors, everything. It felt like it was meant to be." She paused, her faraway gaze clouding with bitterness. "But days before the auction, a distant relative was located. He inherited the property, and that was that. I hoped that by working here and taking a leadership role, I would be in the right place at the right time when the new owner inevitably wanted to sell someday."

"Lankenstein?" Mia guessed out loud, sitting up straighter in the chair.

"Mia!" her mother scolded, though her tone was more amused than stern. "Mr. Murdoch seems like a pleasant man. Be kind."

Before Mia could reply, the sharp slam of a door upstairs made all three women whip their heads toward the sound.

Valentina stood abruptly, her hands smoothing her apron again. "Oh, listen to me ramble. I need to check on dinner. If I leave those boys to finish up, who knows what you'll end up eating."

With an uncomfortable laugh and a brisk bow, she disappeared through the swinging kitchen door.

The sound of rapid footsteps on the stairs filled the silence, followed by Rachel's panicked yell. "Oh my God, Tenner, no!"

CHAPTER EIGHTEEN

Rachel Johnson

NOVEMBER, 2024

Tenner slammed his door shut, the sound echoing through the hall, and leapt down the first ten stairs two at a time. Reaching for the banister, he swung his leg over and slid the rest of the way like a kid on a playground.

From the second-floor landing, Rachel screamed, her voice sharp with panic as she braced for the inevitable catastrophe. She could already picture her brother sprawled at the bottom of the stairs, broken and bleeding. Instead, Tenner landed smoothly, arms raised like a triumphant gymnast. He didn't even glance back at her as he strolled casually into the great room.

Rachel's fear morphed into irritation as she stomped after him. Why was she mad? It wasn't like she *wanted* him to crack his head open. Maybe it was his smug face, his cat-like grace—or the way he always seemed to walk away unscathed.

The great room was bathed in a mix of dim, golden light from low-wattage lamps and the flickering glow of the now-lit fireplace. Mia was curled up in an oversized armchair, bundled like a child in a cocoon of blankets. Tenner, ever the opportunist, had already claimed a spot on the loveseat, lounging as if he'd been there for hours.

Their mom sat in stark contrast. Perched on the center cushion of the sofa, her posture was unnaturally stiff, her gaze distant and unfocused. Something weighed on her mind, and the tension radiated from her like a physical presence.

"Mom," Rachel said as she approached, stopping directly in front of her with her hands firmly planted on her hips. "Tenner slid *all the way* down the railing."

Mia stirred, her head peeking out from her blanket cocoon, and Tenner muttered lazily, "It was only halfway."

Lisa's eyes snapped to life but didn't land on Rachel. Instead, her gaze shifted barely over Rachel's shoulder. A flicker of something—confusion? Fear?—crossed her face.

Rachel frowned. "Mom?"

The atmosphere in the room shifted, like the temperature had dropped a few degrees. Rachel felt it before she saw their reactions: Mia's blanket froze mid-adjustment. Tenner sat up straighter, his relaxed posture gone. Both of them stared at something behind Rachel.

And then she felt it—a breath, warm and too close, brushing the back of her neck. The hairs on her arms stood on end, and her chest tightened with fear. A single tear slipped down her cheek as dread rooted her in place.

Rachel steeled herself and spun around, expecting—*what?*—but finding Manny, standing mere inches away. His face was as blank and impassive as ever, his eyes void of any warmth.

"Dinner is ready," he said in his low, monotone voice.

Rachel's heart pounded in her ears as she stared at him, unable to speak. Manny's expression didn't change as he turned and walked toward the kitchen, his footsteps eerily soft against the hardwood floors.

In the oppressive silence that followed, Tenner muttered, "You scared her to tears, dude."

Rachel exhaled shakily, trying to convince herself that her uneasiness had only been thanks to Manny all along. But the chill lingering in the room told her otherwise.

The long banquet table dominated the back wall, its sheer size making the room feel smaller. Crafted from the same warm wood as much of the lodge's furniture, the smooth, varnished surface showcased its natural imperfections—knots, grain lines, and tiny cracks that only added to its rustic charm. Table length, log-like benches flanked either side, their hard surfaces a less appealing option than the cushioned chairs scattered around the room. Each place setting was carefully arranged with a black stone charger, a simple white plate, and a folded red and black checkered napkin, adding a touch of country flair.

The kitchen door swung open, and Manny reemerged with Jon, each carrying trays laden with food. They moved with practiced ease, setting dishes along the length of the table, interspersed with a fresh pine garland that ran its center. The spread was far more elaborate than Rachel had anticipated for a lodge that felt more B&B than boutique hotel.

Earthenware bowls of varying shapes and colors held seasoned, bite-sized potatoes, a bright, green garden salad, and tender orzo. Oblong clay platters displayed golden-roasted chicken and perfectly grilled asparagus, their presentation bordering on restaurant quality. It was a feast of both taste and aesthetics, and it had Valentina's touch written all over it. The dining setup—cabin chic and effortlessly charming—stood in contrast to the lodge's otherwise ancient, log cabin vibe.

"Perfect timing," their dad called, stepping down the last stair and into the great room. He inhaled deeply. "Wow, something smells incredible!"

Rachel chose a seat midway down the table, her back to the wall giving her a clear view of the great room and the fireplace's golden flames, their shadows flickering across the room. Mia and Tenner claimed the seats on either side of her, while their mom and dad settled in across the table, creating an intimate cluster that left the vast majority of the table empty.

"You'll join us, won't you?" Lisa asked Valentina, her tone warm and inviting as the chef expertly poured a crisp white wine into her glass.

Rachel glanced up in anticipation in time to see Valentina's polite but firm smile. "No, thank you. We only prepare the food."

Behind Valentina, Jon cleared his throat, though whether it was to stifle a laugh or a cough, Rachel couldn't tell.

Valentina moved to their dad's side, wine bottle in hand, but he hovered his palm, face down, over his glass, stopping her before she poured. "None for me, thanks."

Valentina nodded, placing the bottle in a chilled marble vase near Lisa. Her mom, ever quick to explain, whispered with a touch of apology, "Wine can trigger his migraines."

Valentina gave one last look over the table, her sharp eyes scanning for anything amiss. Satisfied, she offered a final nod to the family before retreating into the kitchen with Jon and Manny close behind.

"Awkward," Tenner muttered, leaning over the garland to spear a piece of chicken from the nearest platter.

Rachel's lips twitched in faint amusement, but her attention remained on the empty table space. For all the warmth of the meal, the unspoken divide between their family and the staff lingered. The room dimmed as the sun set, and Rachel recognized that there was something about the look on Valentina's face that was akin to anxiety. *Was she in a rush to get home or was she just in a hurry to leave before dark? The sooner they ate, the sooner she could finish up and get out.*

CHAPTER NINETEEN

Mia Johnson

NOVEMBER, 2024

After several firm refusals of help from the staff, Jon and Manny set to clearing the table while Mia and her family retreated back to the great room. Mia curled up in her chair, tucking the blanket snugly under her feet, while the fire's warmth spread throughout the room.

"I know I've been a bit busy," their mom slurred, clearly trying, and failing, to sound unaffected by the large quantities of wine she'd consumed at dinner. "But how's high school treating you, Tenner?"

"Fine," Tenner answered distractedly, his eyes drifting toward the balcony. Mia could practically see the wheels turning in his head, likely hatching another reckless stunt.

Her gaze shifted to the nearly empty wine bottle on the side table next to her mom. Sensing the conversation needed a nudge, Mia chimed in, "Have you heard about the spooky school history yet?"

Tenner's attention snapped back to his sister, curiosity piqued. "What spooky history?"

"You know," she began, her tone conspiratorial. "The big anti-bullying campaign."

Tenner glanced at Rachel, who nodded from her spot on the couch. "Uh, yeah," she said cautiously.

"Well," Mia continued, "it started about five years ago when the old PTA president, Wanda Skills, decided to tackle the mounting bullying problem. She had a son who was targeted by a couple guys on the basketball team, so it became her mission. She organized orange-themed events and even launched a 'Lunch Buddies' program to pair kids so no one ate alone."

"That's...nice," their mom offered, punctuating the thought with an abrupt hiccup.

Mia shrugged. "Her heart was in the right place, but the program backfired. Some kids got bullied more because of their pairings. Anyway, the rumors say that Ms. Skills snapped. She started by sabotaging the basketball team—soap in their water bottles making them sick, tampering with weight equipment and putting them at risk of injury. Eventually, people got suspicious, and the police began investigating."

Her family leaned in, captivated, the crackling fire adding to the suspense. Even Tenner stopped fidgeting. Mia took a measured sip of water before delivering the climax.

"One day, police stormed into the gym during practice. When they threw open the doors, they found the entire basketball team, two coaches, and a trainer sprawled motionless on the floor, faces frozen in terror, eyes bulging, and lips blue. Standing in front of them, holding a tray of brownies, was Ms. Skills, wearing a floral dress and crisp, white apron. When she turned to face the officers, her wide eyes and twisted smile freaked out a rookie patrolman so badly that he shot her on the spot."

Mia paused to gauge her family's reactions. Her parents had their hands over their mouths, horrified. Rachel looked skeptical, while Tenner seemed utterly enthralled.

"The officer quit, even had to be committed for a while. Ms. Skills' poisoned brownies made her infamous. They say her ghost haunts the gym now, banging on the bleachers when it's empty."

A sudden loud *bang* shattered the moment, sending everyone jumping out of their seats. Mia's heart raced until Jon appeared from the kitchen, looking sheepish. "Sorry," he murmured, hefting two large garbage bags as the door swung shut behind him.

Manny followed with two more bags, and Valentina trailed behind, carrying a storage container. David jumped to his feet to help her.

"Oh, thank you, " Valentina said with a grateful smile. "My car's out front—Mr. Murdoch likes us to park there to make the place look busier."

As David helped carry the container outside, Valentina addressed the family. "Everything's cleaned up, and you should have what you need until morning. If you need anything at all, Manny's staying in the room behind reception. There's a bell on the counter if you need to get his attention."

Mia exchanged smirks with Tenner and Rachel, silently agreeing they'd all be better off if Manny stayed in his room until morning.

"Jon, Matthew, and I will be back for breakfast," Valentina added. Rachel's cheeks flushed noticeably at the mention of Matthew, a reaction that did not go unnoticed by her siblings.

David returned and took his seat as Lisa wobbled to her feet. "I think I'm turning in. See everyone in the morning."

As her mom turned toward the stairs, a sudden scream pierced the room. She froze mid-step, face-to-face with Manny, who stared blankly at her before slow-blinking his eyes and retreating into his room.

"That kid should *wear* a bell," Lisa muttered, climbing the stairs.

CHAPTER TWENTY

Rachel Johnson

NOVEMBER, 2024

Rachel had fully intended to spend at least an hour brainstorming ideas for her essay, but the heavy comfort food and the cozy ambiance of the great room had left her feeling groggy. She plopped down at the small desk in her room, telling herself she could delay the essay until tomorrow. However, she couldn't resist the urge to check her email—her SAT scores were due to be released any day now. Though she felt confident about her performance, she wasn't sure how confident. More than a good score, she craved a perfect one.

Booting up her laptop, she quickly discovered the lodge offered no WiFi service. Worse yet, her phone's cellular signal was nonexistent. She couldn't believe Tenner hadn't raised hell about the lack of service—he practically lived on his phone. Then again, she recalled he'd been watching a downloaded movie earlier, not streaming, making it possible he hadn't realized yet.

With a sigh, Rachel closed her laptop and stood to change into her comfy pajamas. She had no intention of braving the dark halls in the middle of the night to use the bathroom, it was now or never.

Padding out into the hallway, she saw light spilling from beneath the bathroom door. She hesitated, the thought of Manny possibly being upstairs giving her pause. Surely there had to be a downstairs bathroom, right? As she decided to tiptoe back to her room, the door swung open.

Tenner emerged, his shaggy brown hair damp and dripping onto his shoulders, a towel slung low around his waist. He nodded at her with a smirk, his bare feet leaving wet footprints as he confidently strode back to his room.

Rachel exhaled sharply and stepped into the bathroom, determined to be quick. The mirror was fogged from Tenner's shower, the air still humid. Her pulse quickened as memories of earlier that day surfaced—the unsettling feeling of not being alone. She grabbed a hand towel and wiped the mirror, but the streaky surface only partially cleared. Avoiding her own reflection, she crept toward the shower and yanked the curtain back in one swift motion, her breath hitching.

The tub was empty. Her heartbeat slowed slightly.

Satisfied that no one lurked behind the curtain or her reflection, Rachel allowed herself to use the bathroom. But as she washed her hands, she found herself unable to look up. The irrational fear of someone materializing in the foggy mirror paralyzed her. In her mind's eye, she could picture it—a figure standing just behind her, unmoving until she dared to meet its gaze. The thought sent a shiver down her spine.

Without glancing up, she dried her hands, bolted back to her room, and shut the door firmly behind her. Even the most brilliant intellect can find their own imagination both formidable and frightening.

Chapter Twenty-One

Mia Johnson

November, 2024

A faint scratching sound jolted Mia from a deep sleep. The noise, sharp and deliberate, seemed to echo from beneath her bed. Her mind immediately went to the hidden compartment she had discovered earlier—could a mouse have nested there? Or was it something worse? Her imagination, ever restless, leaped to unlikely but unnerving scenarios. She'd read enough unsettling stories to know that "unlikely" didn't mean "impossible."

Without hesitation, Mia leaned over the edge of her bed, her black hair brushing the floor as she peered into the shadowy void underneath. The darkness was thick, unbroken by any flicker of movement. The scratching stopped. For a moment, all was still. She sat back up, her heart beating faster, sleep now a distant memory.

Then came a new sound—a soft, mournful cry, tinged with exhaustion and despair. It was the kind of sound that carried hopelessness, like a wounded animal cornered and helpless, resigned to its fate. Drawn to the window, Mia pulled the curtain aside and scanned the moonlit grounds. But what she saw wasn't an animal.

A figure moved near the edge of the woods. The briefest glimpse revealed the outline of a person, hood pulled tightly over their head, vanishing into the trees before Mia could discern anything more.

Curiosity outweighed caution as Mia stepped toward the door. Slowly, she turned the handle, wincing as the hinges creaked. Slipping into the hallway, she hugged the walls, her feet gliding silently across the floorboards. She descended the stairs carefully, sticking to the outer edges of each step to avoid the creaks—a trick she'd once read in a burglar's memoir.

The person she'd seen could be anyone. Rationally, she knew it wasn't her parents or siblings, but the figure's height and build were impossible to determine from such a distance. The memory of the girl in the window flickered through her mind. Who could she have been? They'd spent half the day at Murdoch Manor, and Mia hadn't seen a single girl. The staff was limited to Valentina and the three guys. So who—or what—was that figure?

Mia opened the front door, surprised by how smoothly and silently it moved on its hinges. Stepping onto the porch, she turned, her bare feet brushing against the cold wood as she approached the end. The frigid mountain air bit at her exposed skin. She looked out toward the woods, but the figure was gone, swallowed by the trees.

Realizing how unprepared she was—no jacket, no shoes, no flashlight, not even her phone—Mia stepped back inside, resolving to investigate further in the morning. Quietly, she shut the door, the latch clicking softly into place.

When she turned, she froze.

Behind the reception desk stood Manny, his pale face illuminated by the faint glow of a nearby lamp. He was dressed in a nondescript t-shirt and flannel pajama pants, no sign of a hoodie or any outdoor wear at all. His emotionless stare was fixed on her, unblinking and unyielding. For a moment, neither moved.

Mia wasn't the type to be easily spooked, but something about the way he watched her rooted her to the spot. The standoff lasted mere seconds before Manny wordlessly turned away and disappeared into his room, the door closing firmly behind him.

Mia exhaled, then climbed the stairs back to her room, her mind swirling with questions she wasn't sure she wanted answered.

Chapter Twenty-Two

Rachel Johnson

November, 2024

Rachel shuffled into the great room, still groggy, only to realize she was the last one to join the morning routine. Mia was already curled up in her usual chair, engrossed in a book featuring the broken, grimy head of an old baby doll on its cover. Rachel shuddered. *How could Mia read that stuff?* Where Rachel shrank from anything remotely frightening, Mia seemed to crave it, as though searching for a thrill that most people felt naturally.

Tenner sat at the dining table, deep in a chess match with their dad, his face alight with satisfaction. The room felt settled—everyone in their element, except for their mom, who sipped a bubbly clear drink while squinting against the light. Overindulging the night before, whether to unwind or avoid waste, clearly hadn't worked out for her.

Valentina appeared from the kitchen, carrying two glass pitchers of juice, followed by Manny and Jon, who balanced trays piled high with coffee cake and danishes. Rachel moved to sit at the table, her mood and appetite dipping slightly at the absence of Matthew.

"Ms. Skills," Tenner muttered, capturing their dad's queen. "Checkmate."

"What did you say?" Rachel asked, distracted.

Her dad tipped over his king and sighed. "He got me again. Always does."

"No, before that," Rachel pressed.

"Ms. Skills," Tenner repeated with a smirk, grabbing a slice of banana bread. "Or should I say, Miss Kills? Nice touch, Mia. You always tell the best ghost stories."

Mia shut her book with deliberate calm, helped their mom to the table, and took a seat.

"None of that story was real, was it?" her mom asked Mia, pouring herself some orange juice.

"Who knows?" Mia asked by way of an answer, her tone perfectly neutral.

Tenner chuckled, leaning back in his chair. "It hit me in the middle of the night—Ms. Skills, Miss Kills. Not that I believed it to begin with. Solid story, though. Did you come up with that, or was it from one of your spooky books?"

Before Mia could respond, Tenner added, "Speaking of last night, I got up to use the bathroom and thought I heard someone on the stairs. Did any of you sneak down for a midnight snack?"

Rachel's eyes flicked to Manny, standing by the kitchen door. She wouldn't put it past him to stalk the halls at night while the guests slept unknowing. His gaze wasn't on her, however. He was looking past her—at

Mia. Rachel turned quickly to catch her sister's expression. She saw it—a flicker of something between them. Not flirtation, though the two did have odd commonalities, but... a shared secret?

"How about a family hike this morning?" their dad suggested, breaking the moment.

"Matthew and Jon can guide you," Valentina offered while refilling glasses.

The mention of Matthew's name sent a wave of relief and excitement through Rachel. She grabbed an apple danish and bit into it hastily, her appetite returning and her mood suddenly brighter.

"You up for that, Rachel?" her dad asked as Matthew emerged from the kitchen. He looked even more polished than the day before, his dark hair slicked back, a black polo tucked neatly into his pressed khakis. Though he was too far away for her to catch his scent, she remembered the clean, woodsy freshness that clung to him the day before.

Every eye in the room turned to Rachel, waiting for her response. With her mouth embarrassingly full of danish, panic set in. Chewing frantically, her eyes watered as she forced the lump of food down with a long gulp of water. She nodded in agreement, avoiding the stares, and wiped at her mouth and eyes.

"The Surinam Toad gives birth through its back.."

Thankful, once again, for Mia's distraction, giving Rachel the opportunity to fully swallow and compose herself, she dared a glance. Her gaze met Matthew's, and one corner of his lips twitched in a half smile. Whether he hadn't noticed her graceless display or was entertained by Mia's unending morbid facts, she couldn't tell.

CHAPTER TWENTY-THREE

Mia Johnson

NOVEMBER, 2024

Matthew and Jon led the way down the winding trail that began at the treeline beside the lodge. Mia and David followed close behind, with David keeping a careful eye on Tenner, who darted ahead whenever something dangerous caught his interest. Bringing up the rear, at a pace more suited to a casual Sunday stroll than a mountain hike, were Lisa and Rachel.

Mia could hear Lisa peppering Rachel with college questions. It was all *extracurriculars this* and *volunteer hours that.* Rachel nodded dutifully, but Mia caught the wistful glance her sister cast toward the front of the group. It was obvious she wanted to walk closer to Matthew.

Mia decided to break the rhythm of chatter. "Is anyone else staying in the lodge?" she asked the brothers as they navigated the winding path.

"Nope," Jon replied. "You've got the whole place to yourselves."

"Is there a girl who works with you?" Mia pressed further, her tone casual but her curiosity sharp.

Matthew stopped abruptly, his posture stiffening as he turned his head slightly. "No. Why do you ask?" he said, his voice slightly defensive.

Sensing the sudden tension, Mia quickly retreated. "No reason," she said with a shrug, filing his reaction away for later and opting to keep the information closer to the vest.

"So, is it just the four of you?" David asked, stepping into the conversation.

Matthew and Jon exchanged a glance, a flicker of something unspoken passing between them. Jon recovered first. "Yes. Our dad passed away a few years ago. Then..."

"Now it's just us three boys and our mom," Matthew interjected smoothly, his tone brightening as he shot a pointed look at Jon.

Mia narrowed her eyes slightly. "So," she said, tilting her head and studying the two distinctly different looking boys. "You two are brothers?"

Matthew let out a laugh, breaking the tension. "We like to joke that Jon is adopted, but the truth is, Manny and I take after our mom, and Jon looks like our dad." He leaned closer to Mia, cupping a hand as if sharing a secret. "His name is actually Juan, but we call him Jon because he looks like a white guy."

Jon rolled his eyes but grinned as Matthew chuckled, the moment easing as Jon gave Matthew a playful punch on the shoulder. "Laugh it up."

"High levels of carbon monoxide or other gasses can induce hallucinations, leading people to believe they are experiencing paranormal activities," Mia blurted out.

With smiles still frozen on their faces, but unsure how to respond, Matthew and Jon quickly glanced at one another before looking back to Mia.

"So, what kind of name is Tenner?" Jon asked, changing the subject.

"Oh," David laughed. "Lisa was so happy with the two girls so I bet her ten dollars that I could give her three. The exact phrase I used was, 'bet you a tenner'. "

Jon laughed. "So, no girl, but you got a 'Tenner' anyway?"

"Something like that," Mia answered, tired of hearing her dad tell the story. She was still surprised when people asked about the origin of Tenner's name. She goes to school with a lot of people with crazy names. It kind of seems like the way it is now. Either way, she wanted to move on to a topic that had been weighing on her.

"Have you ever heard strange noises when you stay overnight?" Mia asked, her voice low but curious. "Seen anything... odd?"

"You think we have a carbon monoxide leak?" Matthew asked, trying to keep the conversation light, nudging Tenner with his elbow.

Jon bent down, feigning fishing a pebble out of his shoe, allowing Matthew, David, and Tenner to continue ahead, their chatter fading as the distance grew. When they were out of earshot, Jon straightened up and fixed Mia with an intense look.

"Look," he said firmly, "Manny told me you went out last night. He wouldn't say anything to stop you. That's not his style. But, I will. Guests should *not* be walking around outside at night."

His protective tone caught Mia off guard. It felt too personal—too concerned—for someone who barely knew her. Why did he care what she did? And why would Manny silently condone it while Jon seemed determined to intervene?

"Why?" she asked, crossing her arms.

Jon let out a frustrated scoff, glancing down as if searching the ground for the right words. "I can't say. Just don't."

"What do you mean, you *can't* say?" she pressed, her curiosity flaring.

He hesitated, then quickly backtracked. "Forget I said that. You're not familiar with the woods or the trails, and in the dark, it's easy to lose your way. That's all. Plus, there are wild animals—most of them nocturnal. It's a liability thing. Just don't go out at night, okay?"

Jon's gaze locked onto hers, searching for a sign of agreement—or at least some measure of acceptance. But Mia's suspicion only deepened.

"You two okay up there?" Lisa's voice called out as she and Rachel approached, their pace quickening to close the gap.

Mia barely had time to respond before Rachel seized the opportunity to escape Lisa's scrutiny. She jogged forward, leaving Lisa to hover near Mia and Jon as the others disappeared up the trail.

Mia bit her lip, casting one last look at Jon. His unease was palpable, urging her to keep quiet. For now, he seemed unwilling—or unable—to explain.

Chapter Twenty-Four

Rachel Johnson

November, 2024

"Most men experience an erection at high altitudes."

Rachel barely registered Mia's fading voice as she hurried to catch up with her dad—and more importantly, Matthew. The trail was uneven, her tennis shoes ill-suited for the terrain, but she slowed enough to steady her breathing. She hung back, close enough to hear their conversation but far enough to remain undetected.

"...so many extreme sports junkies in the mountains," Matthew was saying to an awestruck Tenner.

Rachel quickened her pace, determined to join them without tripping over her nerves—or her feet. Unfortunately, the exposed root of a tree had other plans. Her toe snagged, and she went down hard, hands outstretched to keep her face from smacking the dirt.

"Are you okay, honey?" her dad asked, crouching beside her and rubbing her back.

"I'm fine!" she snapped, louder than intended. Her embarrassment flared hotter than the sting in her scraped palms. She hesitated, praying Matthew wasn't laughing at her. But when she raised her eyes, he wasn't there. And, neither was Tenner.

The absence of Tenner's usual mocking laughter hit her harder than the fall. Rachel stood, brushing herself off despite her dad's efforts to help. Her toe throbbed, her wrists ached, but a chill ran through her that had nothing to do with the cold breeze whispering through the skeletal branches.

"Dad, where's Tenner?" she asked, her voice barely audible. The long path in front of them was vacant for as far as Rachel could see. She scanned the forest, but the dense patchwork of trees and underbrush limited her view.

Her mom, Mia, and Jon approached from behind.

"What are you two up to?" her mom asked lightly, though the tension in Rachel's posture quickly darkened the mood.

"Where's Tenner?" Rachel asked again, her voice sharper.

"Where's Matthew?" Mia and Jon asked simultaneously. Their unease mirrored Rachel's.

Rachel's mother cupped her hands around her mouth and shouted, "Tenner!"

"Over here!" Tenner's voice called from somewhere off the path.

Relief flooded Rachel, but it was short-lived. Jon muttered a curse under his breath, his face pale and frozen, his eyes wide and unblinking. His easy-going persona was gone— leaving him coiled tight like a spring.

Then he moved, launching into a full sprint toward the sound of Tenner's voice. Rachel barely had time to think before she followed, dodging snapping branches and clawing underbrush. Her injured toe throbbed with every step, but she didn't slow down.

When she finally broke into a clearing, Jon was already there, standing a few yards away. Tenner and Matthew were at the edge of the cliff, leaning precariously over the vast nothingness. Rachel froze, her breath catching in her throat.

"What are you doing?" she called, her voice cracking.

Neither Tenner nor Matthew turned. They stared down into the abyss, motionless, as if something unseen by Rachel had their full attention.

And then Tenner spoke, his voice flat and unnervingly calm. "There's something down there."

Chapter Twenty-Five

Sal Boatwright

January, 1966

The tail end of hunting season had arrived, and Sal Boatwright was forcing himself to follow through on a promise he had made to himself. His shotgun had been cleaned and polished a dozen times over the past month, his camouflage laid out more times than he could count. But each time he considered stepping out the door, an invisible weight anchored him in place.

Margaret had been his hunting partner for decades. Now, she's gone.

They just celebrated their fifty-first wedding anniversary when she was taken from him—suddenly, without warning. A massive heart attack in the middle of their quiet living room. One moment, she was there, teasing him about his thinning hair, and the next...

Nearly a year had passed, and he still didn't understand how his own heart hadn't given out from the sheer weight of his grief. But somehow, every morning, he woke up.

George, his next-door neighbor and a fellow widower, had been a lifeline in ways Sal hadn't expected. He stopped by with takeout when he knew Sal hadn't eaten, left fresh flowers from his garden on the porch, and sat with him in silence on the hard winter nights. Lately, though, his kindness had shifted to something more akin to tough-love.

"Margaret would want you to live your life, not just survive," George had said over coffee one morning. "The pain won't go away, but you'll enjoy life more if you do something that would make her proud."

Sal had scoffed at first, but George's words burrowed into him, took root. He started going to the senior center for bingo night, forcing himself into conversations. He even made plans to start a garden in the spring—Margaret's favorites: tomatoes, zucchini, bell peppers.

But the real challenge, the one that had been gnawing at him, was hunting. Alone.

That's how he found himself here, parked on the side of a rural road, gripping the steering wheel so hard his knuckles turned white and began to ache. If he could get out of the truck, that would be the first step.

Eventually, he did.

The hike into the woods was harder than he remembered. His joints protested with every step, his breath coming shorter than it used to. Margaret's voice echoed in his mind, reminding him to stay hydrated, to be alert.

The forest was alive in its own way—branches swayed, leaves whispered, unseen animals scurried through the underbrush. He followed a well-worn deer path, noting fresh scat nearby, and settled into a natural blind of brush. His thermals and quilted camo did little to fend off the creeping chill that gnawed at his bones.

Then—movement.

The sound of hooves sent a jolt through him, and he raised his shotgun, lining up the bead sight to the direction from where the noise was coming. Any second now, a deer or even a herd would break through the foliage. He braced himself.

But the sound stopped.

Nothing moved. No deer emerged.

Sal's pulse quickened. He kept his shotgun raised, scanning the trees. Then, beyond a tangle of branches, he saw them—a doe, two fawns, and behind them, a massive fifteen-point buck.

A trophy.

Habit tempted him to look at his ever-present wife and celebrate their luck, but his sad reality combined with his hunting instinct kept his eyes forward.

The buck stood alert, muscles taut, nostrils flaring. But it wasn't looking at Sal. None of the deer were.

All four were staring at something over his shoulder.

A strange sensation crawled up his spine. His instincts screamed at him to look, but the hunter in him resisted. He had a clean shot if he waited a little longer. Another few inches, and he could take the buck down clean.

He no longer felt the urge to look over to empty space that used to be occupied by the love of his life, but the increasing temptation to search for a threat, and prepare to defend himself.

A bead of sweat rolled down his temple. His palms grew slick. The fawn twitched, shifting nervously. The doe's ears flicked back. The buck's breath plumed in the cold air, but he didn't move a muscle.

Sal swallowed hard. The feeling—the *wrongness*—was overpowering now.

Slowly, he pulled back from the sight, wiped his forehead. And then, against every hunter's instinct, he turned.

A figure stood not quite twenty feet away, head to toe in cold-weather hunting gear, a rifle aimed directly at *him*.

Sal's breath hitched. His muscles locked, then jerked into motion all at once. He rocked back, his stiff legs giving out beneath him, sending him sprawling onto his backside. His shotgun slipped from his grasp, landing in the frostbitten leaves.

But his eyes never left the rifle.

The figure didn't move. Not at first. But somehow, the barrel seemed to get closer, inch by inch, breath by breath.

"Not a deer," Sal rasped, his voice hoarse and absurd in the vast silence.

The figure didn't react.

A hunter wouldn't do this. A hunter would call out, explain themselves. This wasn't a mistake. Sal could feel it in his bones.

This was a predator.

Adrenaline overrode aching bones and exhaustion. Sal scrambled to his feet, spun on instinct, and bolted toward the deer trail.

A shot cracked through the trees.

He flinched, covering his head, then veered sharply, branches lashing at his face, roots snaring his boots. He ran faster than he had in years, his breath burning in his lungs. He needed an escape—somewhere to hide, a way to lose his pursuer.

Then, up ahead, a clearing.

Relief surged through him. If he could just break through...

But when he did, he skidded to a stop, toes barely clinging to solid ground.

The earth ended.

A sheer drop stretched before him, the cliff face plummeting into jagged rocks below.

Sal's heart pounded against his ribs as he turned, hands raised in surrender. His hunter emerged from the tree line, moving slow now, deliberate. The rifle never wavered.

"P-please," Sal stammered. "I'm a hunter."

The figure stepped closer.

Sal saw the muzzle flash.

The blast slammed into his chest, and the world tilted—leaving Sal with nothing to look at but the overcast winter sky as he fell, dying well before his body hit the jagged rocks below.

CHAPTER TWENTY-SIX

Mia Johnson

NOVEMBER, 2024

As Mia brought up the rear, trailing her parents who sprinted through the woods after Rachel, the sound of Tenner's distant call guiding their frantic pace. Branches clawed at her sleeves, and her breath frosted in the cold air. When they broke into the clearing, an unsettling mix of uncomfortable laughter and sharp voices greeted them.

"You could've killed me!" Rachel shrieked, her voice cracking with anger and lingering fear.

"Get away from that ledge right now!" Lisa barked at the three figures precariously close to the cliff's edge.

"What were you thinking, Tenner?" David snapped, his tone more scolding than concerned. "Running off like that? Imagine if you had accidentally walked off the edge?"

Tenner, standing awkwardly near the edge, looked genuinely remorseful. "Matthew wanted to show me the deer graveyard," he mumbled, his voice small.

"I've listened to enough true crime to know human remains are often mistaken as animals in the wild," David interjected enthusiastically, appearing much less concerned with the danger to his family than the opportunity to find himself in his own mystery.

Rachel turned on him, her face flushed and trembling. "Dad!" she screamed, "When I looked, Tenner pretended to push me off!" Her voice cracked again, and tears welled in her eyes.

For a moment, Mia's eyes shifted to Matthew. She could've sworn she caught a fleeting smile on his lips, smug and unbothered, but it vanished almost instantly. He slung a gentle arm around Rachel's shoulders, his expression softening into one of pity.

"We didn't mean to scare you," Matthew said, his voice low and soothing. He tilted his head so far down he had to look up to meet Rachel's teary gaze, his eyes wide and apologetic, almost puppy-like.

"I thought Tenner would find it interesting," Matthew continued. "This is a place where deer must run off the ledge or something. I figured he'd want to see it." A dark lock of hair fell over his eyes as he raised a corner of his mouth in a faint, sheepish smile, as though silently asking for forgiveness.

Mia rolled her eyes and strode toward the cliff before Lisa could stop her. When she leaned out to peer into the gorge, her stomach clenched. There were no deer carcasses or animal remains scattered below—just a stark pile of bones, bleached white and picked clean.

"What makes you think they're deer?" Mia asked, her voice sharper than intended as she turned back to face Matthew.

Matthew shrugged, letting his arm drop from Rachel's tense shoulders. "What else could they be? They're too big to be squirrels or foxes, and I don't think bears or wolves are dumb enough to run off a cliff."

Mia frowned at his answer. "Neither are deer," she muttered under her breath as she stepped away.

Lisa called after her, but Mia didn't stop. She pushed through the brush with a brisk pace, her thoughts racing faster than her feet. Matthew's explanation didn't sit right with her, and she didn't need a lecture to know why. Deer were too instinctual, too finely attuned to their environment to stumble off something as fatal as a cliff. Spooked or not, they wouldn't leap to their deaths. Deer weren't lemmings after all.

She could hear the others catching up, but she didn't look back. Something about Matthew bothered her—giving her a sneaky, unshakable feeling. That fleeting smirk when Rachel was terrified wasn't just disturbing—it was revealing. Matthew wasn't the easygoing charmer he pretended to be.

Mia didn't trust him.

Rachel, clearly infatuated, wouldn't listen to her even if Mia tried to warn her. So she decided to keep her suspicions to herself for now and watch. Manny might be strange but he wore his oddities on his sleeve like a badge of honor. But Matthew? He was more dangerous. The kind of dangerous that hid behind a polished grin and kind words—a wolf in sheep's clothing. And that was far, far worse.

Chapter Twenty-Seven

Rachel Johnson

November, 2024

Little conversation passed between the family for the rest of the afternoon. They sat together through a near-silent lunch of fresh bread and deli meats, and later gathered in the cavernous great room, but the atmosphere was thick with unspoken tension. Each kept to themselves.

Mia wore headphones, swaying slightly to her music, while Tenner hunched over his tablet, watching yet another downloaded movie. Their dad lounged in his chair, nodding along to what Rachel could only assume was another true crime podcast. He tore through episodes—listening at home, in the car, even on his phone. Apparently, he'd had the foresight to download a bunch before heading into the signal-free mountains. Rachel had often caught snippets when he picked her up from school and wondered how he could stomach something so morbid. Her eyes drifted back to Mia. *Guess the apple doesn't fall far...*

Rachel, on the other hand, wore noise-canceling headphones in a weak attempt to block out the world. Her laptop sat open in front of her, the cursor blinking on a blank page that seemed to mock her.

Her mother, oblivious to the suffocating weight of her earlier comments about college essays, sat by the window sipping a generous glass of wine. Did her mom not understand how much Rachel already had on her plate? Grades, extracurriculars, volunteer hours, the essay—*all of it*—was a ticking time bomb of expectations. She needed to write something groundbreaking, something no other applicant in the history of college admittance had written. Every time her mom brought it up, Rachel's stress ratcheted higher.

But the essay wasn't the only thing clouding her mind. The first boy to ever make her feel…anything, had seen her fall *twice* since they arrived. And then she'd nearly burst into tears, convinced she was going to tumble over the edge of that cliff. What could Matthew possibly think of her now? Whether she'd blown her chance with him or not, the thought of him consumed her. His absence only made it worse—since they returned from the hike, neither he nor his family had been around.

After lunch, Rachel freshened up, and even put on a swipe of mascara, in case she ran into him. But hours had passed, and she'd seen no sign of Matthew—or his brothers. She couldn't shake the feeling that there were secret passageways in the lodge, hidden routes the staff used to stay out of sight. It was impossible for them to spend their entire day in the kitchen. Wasn't it?

An hour of staring blankly at her screen passed before her laptop battery died. Right on cue, Valentina stepped out of the kitchen, her apron crisp and clean.

"Dinner is ready," she announced with a pleasant smile.

Rachel closed her laptop and stretched. Her muscles ached, whether from the hike or from hours spent hunched over, she wasn't sure. The five of them rose and shuffled tentatively toward the dining area. The table, set as beautifully as the night before, gleamed under the soft light of the chandelier. Rachel frowned in confusion, realizing she hadn't observed anyone leaving the kitchen to prepare it.

As they sat, Tenner broke the silence. "So, Mia," he asked, grinning. "No cool facts about deer cliff-diving?"

Without missing a beat, Mia replied, "No, but according to cannibals, the human eye is the most delicious part of the body."

"Mia!" their mom scolded sharply before regaining her composure. "Not at the table."

"No deer facts, then?" Tenner teased, feigning disappointment.

The kitchen door swung open, interrupting their banter. The three boys emerged, balancing platters piled high with food. The rich aroma of pasta, garlic, and fresh herbs filled the air, momentarily lifting the mood. Meatballs, noodles, salad, and warm garlic bread were set in the center of the table. The sight was enough to give Rachel a spark of hope that maybe, with the setting sun, there was still a chance to salvage the day.

But her optimism fizzled quickly. Without so much as a word or smile, Matthew and his brothers turned and disappeared back into the kitchen.

"Enjoy," Valentina said with a small bow before following her sons out.

"Wow," their mom whispered, picking up her fork. "I wish Valentina and her boys could live with us year-round."

Tenner glanced at Rachel, his mouth full of a half-chewed meatball, his expression screaming mischief. But before his sarcastic remark could escape, Rachel kicked his shin hard under the table.

"Don't," she hissed, glaring at him.

Tenner winced but held his tongue, his lips twitching with suppressed laughter. Rachel's gaze flicked toward the kitchen door. The food smelled incredible, but the absence of the boys left a strange hollowness in the room.

Chapter Twenty-Eight

Rachel Johnson

November, 2024

The ceiling above Rachel's bed was a strange mosaic of time. The newer white paint was smooth in places, but the textures beneath it told a different story—a mix of cracks, uneven surfaces, and remnants of the worn popcorn style that had been popular long ago. Staring up at it, Rachel thought it looked like an ancient geometric rock, chipped and weathered. Her restless mind drifting anywhere other than the anxious thoughts of college applications and hopeful daydreams of Matthew.

Instead of counting sheep, she traced the ceiling's imperfections with her eyes, trying to find shapes as one might in the clouds. So far, she'd managed only an amoeba. Time seemed meaningless—she wasn't any closer to sleep than when she first crawled under the covers.

A sharp tapping broke the heavy silence of her room.

Rachel froze. The sound wasn't random—it wasn't quite rhythmic either, but its frequency was increasing, a staccato beat that matched her quickening heartbeat. Her breath hitched as the noise grew louder, more insistent.

Unable to bear it any longer, she leapt from the bed and dashed to the door. Gripping the knob, she yanked it with all her strength, but it didn't budge. The unexpected resistance threw her off balance, and she tumbled backward, hitting the floor with a thud.

Scrambling to her feet, Rachel's hands fumbled for the lock. She twisted the cold metal turnkey, pulled again, and this time the door flew open.

Rachel stepped into the hallway but came to an abrupt halt.

Mia stood directly in front of her door, her face pale and eyes wide. She wasn't looking at Rachel, however. Her gaze was fixed on the base of the stairwell, unblinking and glassy. A chill raced down Rachel's spine as she followed Mia's line of sight.

At the bottom of the stairs stood Jon, his face stern and his brows furrowed. He wasn't moving, only staring up at them with an unsettling intensity. He slowly shook his head with a subtle, deliberate motion. The movement, though soundless, echoed an internal scream in Rachel's head. "NO!"

Rachel's heart thudded against her ribcage. She almost wished she'd caught her reclusive sister sneaking out for a secret rendezvous—it would've been shocking, sure, but it would have been *normal*. This, however, was far from normal and the look the two exchanged was anything but romantic.

Mia didn't move, her arms limp at her sides, her body unnervingly still. Jon, standing like a prison guard at the base of the stairs, seemed more like a warning than a person.

"Go back to bed," Mia said softly, her voice detached, as though she were speaking from a dream. She didn't glance at Rachel or even flinch at her sudden appearance.

"Mia, I'm scared," Rachel whispered, the words slipping out before she could stop them.

Mia turned her head toward her older sister, her expression softening. "Did you hear it too?"

"Yes, the tapping," Rachel said, her voice trembling. "It kept getting faster and faster, and then... "

She stopped as Mia's face shifted, confusion crossing her features.

"Oh," Mia said, almost disappointed. "That's just the rain. Honestly, I can't believe it's not snowing."

"Wait," Rachel interrupted, panic rising. "What sound were *you* talking about?"

Mia's gaze drifted back to the stairwell. Jon was gone. The space he'd occupied a heavy darkness, as though his presence had left behind something intangible but menacing.

"Do you want me to sleep in your room?" Mia asked suddenly, her voice uncharacteristically tender.

Rachel blinked in surprise. Her sister was rarely this kind, often dismissive actually, especially when it came to fear. The unexpected gentleness was almost as unsettling as everything else, but Rachel didn't care. She couldn't be alone.

"Please," she said, stepping back into her room and holding the door open for Mia.

Mia followed without hesitation, settling onto the edge of the bed. Rachel slid under the quilt, her body trembling.

The tapping sound was clearer now, obviously raindrops on the roof. How had she thought it was something else? Her mind must have been playing tricks on her.

Even with Mia sitting near, Rachel couldn't shake the unease that clung to her like a second skin. She reached out, her fingers brushing her sister's hand, and Mia clasped it without hesitation.

"One in fifty people in the US have a brain aneurysm that just hasn't ruptured, but one does rupture every eighteen minutes."

Only then did Rachel close her eyes, though her sleep would be anything but peaceful.

CHAPTER TWENTY-NINE

Mia Johnson

NOVEMBER, 2024

Mia desperately needed a shower after the restless night she'd spent with Rachel. Their shared body heat had turned the bed into a sauna, but as her feet touched the icy floor, a shiver raced up her spine. The chill was so sharp that even the thought of stepping out of a hot shower onto cold tiles made her second-guess the effort. She grabbed an oversized black hoodie and a pair of thick, fluffy socks from her room and quietly shuffled downstairs, surprised her breath wasn't visible in the crisp morning air.

The scene outside the great room window was breathtakingly harsh. The world beyond the frost-kissed glass sparkled with a sheet of silver. Frost clung to every branch and blanketed the gravel driveway, turning it into a shimmering path of ice. The rain from the night before had frozen, and the biting cold had sharpened every edge of her memory.

Mia's thoughts drifted back to the eerie moaning cry she'd heard again in the dead of night. It echoed faintly in her mind—a mournful wail that chilled her more than the frigid floor. It could have been the wind twisting through the trees or the creak of a branch under the weight of ice. But deep down, she knew it was something else. Something human. Something broken.

Her curiosity had driven her to investigate. She'd crept to the top of the stairs, straining to hear the sound more clearly, but Jon had been there, standing guard at the base. His presence was both warning and menace, and his slow, deliberate shake of the head was enough to freeze her in place. His cautionary words from their hike—about the dangers of the woods at night—echoed in her mind. Yet, he never explained the real reason for his unease. But more frightening than the gentle giant's menacing posture, was the surprised look on the face of the girl who hid behind him.

The girl was a wisp of a being, so small behind Jon's hulking frame that Mia could almost convince herself she was imagining things or that maybe even her eyes were playing tricks on her in the dark. But the pleading she felt as she locked eyes with the girl was undeniable.

When Rachel burst out of her room, startled and afraid, Mia had expected her to comment on Jon's strange behavior, but the fact that she didn't mention Jon or more importantly the strange girl hovering behind his back, told Mia all she needed to know. Rachel hadn't seen the girl and more likely than not, neither had Jon. Suddenly, the fact that no one else witnessed the girl in the window when they arrived made sense.

This wasn't the first time Mia saw things that no one else did, but previous sightings were always brief glimpses or sudden movements out of the corner of her eye that took human form but gave her no discerning details. This girl was solid and had stared back at her.

Rachel was oblivious, claiming she was frightened of the rain—a laughable excuse under normal circumstances, but last night, Mia had felt an unfamiliar pang of empathy. Maybe it was the sight of the girl who'd aroused the feelings, but she knew Rachel needed her. She'd stayed with her sister, holding her hand until she drifted back to sleep, ears straining for the agonizing wail or Jon's footsteps on the stairs. Within a few hours, as the house remained eerily silent, she'd finally succumbed to exhaustion.

Now, sitting in the great room, too cold to consider a shower, the warmth of the fire pulled her back to the present. She wrapped herself in a blanket, the flickering flames casting long, shifting shadows across the room. She tried to relax, but unease taunted her. The fire meant someone else was awake—likely Jon. She scanned the room, her eyes scanning the corners where the shadows seemed to take on sinister shapes.

BAM!

The front door slammed open, and a gust of frigid air roared through the room, extinguishing the fragile warmth. Mia's heart leaped into her throat. She half-expected to see Jon storming in, but the door swayed on its hinges, creaking in the icy wind.

Her pulse raced as she stood and edged closer, her cold toes curling inside her socks against the frosty floor. The door swung gently, pushed and pulled by the wind, until another gust slammed it fully open again. She was only a step away from grabbing the handle when a massive, gloved hand appeared from the other side.

Mia jumped back as a large figure stepped through, covered head to toe in thick snow gear. The man moved deliberately, closing the door behind him and stomping his boots on the mat, sending clumps of ice chunks flying. When he pulled back his hood and tugged down his balaclava, Jon's fiery red hair sprang free, sticking up with static electricity.

"A cockroach can live over a week without a head," Mia called out in an attempt to hide her shock.

"Holy shit!" he exclaimed, spotting Mia standing there, wide-eyed and pale. His initial shock melted into a warm, boyish grin. "I didn't think anyone was up."

He hung his coat and scarf on the rack with practiced ease, his demeanor as casual as if nothing had happened the night before. "I was salting the porch and steps," he said, his back to her. "Wouldn't want anyone to fall."

The words were innocent enough, but they struck Mia like a cold blade. She stared at him, trying to reconcile this friendly, laid-back version of Jon with the haunted figure who had blocked her descent the previous night. When he turned to face her, his pale face was flushed red from the cold, his grin genuine.

"You know, your sister?" he added, as if explaining further. "She's a little clumsy, right? Better safe than sorry."

Before Mia could respond, the sound of an engine rumbled outside—a low, guttural roar that grew louder. She rushed to the window, half-expecting some monstrous vehicle to come crashing through the lodge. Instead, she saw a pickup truck roll up the drive, its rusted body and oversized tires giving it a post-apocalyptic appearance. Thick plumes of exhaust billowed into the frosty air, clouding the view.

The front door swung open again, and this time, Valentina entered, flanked by Matthew and Manny, all carrying armloads of grocery bags. Valentina's cheerful voice cut through the tension. "Good morning, Mia! I hope Trevor's truck didn't wake you." She waved to the unseen driver before shutting the door firmly behind her. "Our little car would've never made it up the mountain this morning. Our sweet neighbor is kind enough to give us a ride on days like this. Unfortunately, the ice is only going to get worse today."

Mia watched them, her unease simmering beneath the surface. Valentina exchanged warm words with Jon in Spanish, pinching his cheek affectionately before bustling off to the kitchen. Jon's demeanor remained light, but Mia couldn't shake the lingering chill—not from the cold, but from the warning in his eyes the night before.

CHAPTER THIRTY

Rachel Johnson

NOVEMBER, 2024

The first thing Rachel felt was the stillness of the room, a quiet calm broken only by the faint clattering of glassware from downstairs. She stretched, the quilt slipping off her shoulder, and immediately noted the absence of Mia. Waking alone after clinging to her sister all night should have been unnerving, but Rachel felt a surprising optimism as sunlight poured through the frost-etched windows. The fears of the previous night seemed distant and childish under the bright glow of morning.

Still, before she made her way to the bathroom, she'd wanted to grab her mom before she headed downstairs in hopes of rationalizing the noises in the night. Rachel knew if she brought it up around her dad, the conversation would turn dark, surely leading to some wild theory about crimes of the past. His crime-fueled mind tended to veer toward worst case scenarios. Her mom, on the other hand, was logical and more likely to downplay Rachel's concerns—exactly what she needed.

It only took a few steps towards her parent's room for Rachel to hear that behind the door, her mom was on a business call, yelling into the phone as if the increase in her volume would somehow overcompensate for the spotty cellular service. Whether they were on a family vacation or enjoying a nice dinner at the end of a long day, her mother could never unplug. Her phone was a permanent fixture in her hand, and it wasn't unusual for her to leave mid-meal to take a call. The stress of her job combined with supporting the family and caring for who she often described as her *four kids* was taking its toll. Not only was she spending less time with the family, but her hair was greying, she'd gained weight, and her previously-charming smile lines in the corners of her eyes were now overshadowed by distinct scowl lines etched into her forehead. Bringing up strange noises to her mom, in her current over-stressed state, would most likely result in a public shaming at breakfast. Rachel opted to head to the bathroom instead.

A long, hot shower followed and for once, she didn't find herself glancing nervously at the fogged-up mirror or behind the closed curtain. The steady stream of warm water felt like a small victory, washing away the tension that had knotted her muscles. Dressed in cozy layers, Rachel made her way downstairs, drawn by the aroma of something delicious along with the inviting warmth of the great room.

The scene could have been plucked from a holiday postcard: a roaring fire casting a golden glow, its warmth offsetting the seasonal beauty of icicles hanging from the roofline. Mia was curled up in her favorite chair, her silhouette framed by the flickering flames. At the large table, Tenner and her mom sat feasting on a spread of bagels, muffins, and crumbly coffee cakes. The atmosphere was surprisingly cheerful, almost festive, as though the stormy tension of the previous day had melted with the frost on the windows.

Matthew emerged from the kitchen carrying a pitcher of orange juice and a carafe of coffee, his presence commanding the room without effort. His black polo and khaki pants seemed impossibly crisp for someone working at a rustic lodge, but it was his warm smile that caught Rachel off guard. The way his dark, almond-shaped eyes met hers made her heart flutter. She tucked a strand of her wet hair behind her ear and looked away before anyone noticed her staring.

"Good morning, Rachel," Matthew said, his voice low and smooth as he leaned to pour juice into her glass. The faint scent of his cologne—clean, woodsy, with a hint of spice—wafted toward her, and Rachel's thoughts scrambled. How could someone smell that good this early in the morning?

Before she could respond, Jon entered the room—his red hair wild with static—carrying a bottle of champagne. Seeing him reminded Rachel of the strange events from the night before, but in the daylight, the image of him standing like a junkyard dog at the stairs struck her as more amusing than menacing. Surely, his caution had been more about her siblings sneaking around than anything sinister. Her gaze refocused on Matthew as he approached Jon.

"Jeez, Rachel," Tenner's voice snapped her from her thoughts. "Stalk much?"

Heat rushed to her cheeks as she was caught staring after Matthew again as he pushed through the door to the kitchen. "Shut up," she muttered, sinking into her seat and focusing on smearing cream cheese onto her bagel.

Valentina breezed into the room as if stepping onto a stage, her energy instantly commanding attention. "Good morning, Johnson family!" she sang, her polished appearance as impeccable as ever despite the early hour.

The table chorused their greetings, Rachel's dad joining them after a lively jog down the stairs. "Another amazing spread, Valentina." He pulled his headphones off one ear as he leaned over the table deciding where to start. "If you all don't mind, I'm going to take my breakfast to the front porch and finish the episode I'm listening to. Then, it's family hike time!"

After picking up a bagel and smearing half with cream cheese, he turned to find Valentina blocking his path. "How do you listen to those horrible things?"

Valentina shook her head and tutted, the disappointment in her voice making him shrink away.

"Murder, kidnapping, rape? Isn't it all horribly depressing? And, what about the families of the victims? Your entertainment, at what cost?"

Rachel's dad froze temporarily, before a warm smile spread across his face as if he'd waited his whole life to explain the merits of his hobby. "It's not all tragedy, Valentina. There is redemption, vindication, and closure. Yes, bad guys do bad things, but when the good guys get the answers and solve crimes, there is justice."

Valentina stepped aside to let him pass, her gaze dropping to the floor. "Not all crimes are solved, Mr. Johnson."

The formal nature of her address was like a slap across the face, wiping his smile away.

"Not all families get closure," Valentina continued.

Rachel looked around the table. Even Tenner froze mid-chew.

"You know, you're right, Valentina," her dad's calm voice and decision not to debate the issue allowed Rachel's shoulders to relax and for all at the table to finally exhale. "We're on vacation. I don't want to bring down the mood. Let's all eat together and get to the hike."

Rachel watched as her dad stepped over the bench taking a seat next to her mom. He placed his bagel back down and reached for an already-poured glass of orange juice. But his face twisted into a grimace after taking a long sip. "Ugh, I just brushed my teeth."

"Oh no," her mom exclaimed, looking at her own glass in horror. "David, you drank my mimosa!"

Her dad froze, the realization dawning with a mix of panic and resignation. "Wait... how much was champagne?" he asked, smacking his lips like someone testing for poison.

Her mom winced, her voice small. "Maybe a splash of orange juice?"

With a theatrical groan, her dad clutched his temples and slumped into his seat. Rachel rolled her eyes at the all-too-familiar routine. His migraines were a family joke—less a medical certainty and more a self-fulfilling prophecy. Had he drunk her mom's mimosa and not known, would it have affected him at all?

Valentina, ever unfazed, offered a bright distraction. "It's icy out there," she warned. "I'd suggest staying inside, but if you do venture out, let me know. My boys can fetch some ice spikes for your shoes."

Tenner groaned. "If dad has a migraine, there is no way mom will let us go on a hike. Plus, no internet this morning. Again. What are we supposed to do all day?"

Valentina's expression brightened. "We've got a cabinet full of board games in the sitting room off the lobby. I'll have the boys show you after breakfast." She disappeared as gracefully as she'd entered, leaving Rachel to eye the doorway longingly.

The thought of spending the day in the sitting room, maybe even playing games with Matthew, was enough to make her want to rush through her meal. For now, though, she bit into her bagel and tried to play it cool, even as excitement bubbled just below the surface.

CHAPTER THIRTY-ONE

Mia Johnson

NOVEMBER, 2024

Mia trailed behind the others into the sitting room, the weight of second-hand embarrassment pressing on her shoulders as Rachel practically floated alongside Matthew, her starry-eyed expression as obvious as a neon sign. Mia cringed inwardly—her sister looked like a lovesick puppy, and Matthew's polite but oblivious demeanor wasn't helping.

The room surprised her. She had expected something stiff and old-fashioned, maybe a somber place with high-backed antique chairs and lace doilies where people exchanged pleasantries in hushed tones. Instead, the "sitting room" was a full-blown game room. In the center sat a large poker table surrounded by six plush, rolling office chairs that practically invited you to flop down and stay a while. The front wall boasted the same towering windows as the great room, offering a clear view of the porch and the icicles glinting as they melted in the afternoon sun. The back wall was dominated by an enormous bookshelf, which, rather than holding dusty tomes of classic literature, was crammed with an eclectic collection of board games. Some were old, their boxes worn and frayed, while others looked pristine, as if they'd been purchased yesterday and forgotten.

"So," Matthew began, gesturing at the shelves like a showman unveiling a prize. "As you can see, we've got quite the selection here."

He dropped into a chair at the poker table, flashing a grin at Rachel as he added, "Maybe tonight, when the adults are asleep, we can play a friendly game of poker."

The flush on Rachel's face was immediate, her cheeks reddening so deeply that Mia worried steam might start rising from her sister's head. By her dazed expression, Mia figured Rachel's mind had already leapt to *strip* poker, while Matthew, utterly clueless, shuffled a deck of cards with a practiced ease.

Jon, seated on Matthew's other side, began doling out chips with the air of a seasoned dealer. "Quick card lesson first, then we'll find a board game to play."

Tenner slid into the seat next to Rachel, his face lit by the faint glow of his perpetually useless phone. "Let me guess," he drawled, tossing his phone onto the table when it failed to find service yet again. "You guys are secretly card sharks hired to fleece unsuspecting tourists out of their life savings?"

Jon's booming laugh was surprisingly warm, easing the tension in the room. Mia let herself relax enough to claim a seat, though her curiosity was piqued when Jon turned toward the lobby and called, "Manny, you in?"

Manny appeared in the lobby outside the doorway, one foot poised on the first step of the staircase, arms stacked high with towels. He paused, offering an exaggerated eye roll before resuming his climb. The unexpected display of sass caught Mia off guard, and a small laugh bubbled out of her before she could stop it.

It only took one round of play for Jon and Matthew to realize the siblings didn't need a lesson—Christmases spent playing poker with cousins, using cereal as stakes, had prepared them well.

As Matthew shuffled the deck again, a soft *ding* from his phone on the table drew Mia's attention. He quickly flipped the phone over, but not before she caught a glimpse of the screen. The photo used as his screensaver featured his family—a younger version of the three brothers, their mother, and a man she assumed was their father. But what made her breath catch was the girl standing in front of the boys. It was the same girl Mia had seen hiding behind Jon the night before.

"Service!" Tenner shouted, shattering the moment. He knocked over a stack of chips in his haste to snatch up his phone. Mia pocketed two, ten dollar poker chips in his distraction.

Matthew chuckled, a touch of tension in his voice. "Yeah, it comes and goes up here."

Mia bit her lip, itching to pepper him with questions about the girl in the photo. But she knew better—her previous attempt on the hike to ask about the girl she'd seen in the window had been shut down with unnerving finality. She'd have to be more subtle.

Her gaze wandered to the bookshelves, scanning for a game that might act as an icebreaker, when she noticed Rachel sitting stiffly, her eyes downcast. Clearly, Rachel hadn't seen the photo, but she must have misinterpreted Matthew's quick reaction as proof he had a girlfriend. The thought seemed to extinguish her earlier excitement, leaving her looking crestfallen.

"Dogs like squeaky toys because they mimic the screams of their prey," Mia blurted out before an idea sparked in her mind, bold and unbidden. "Truth or dare," she followed. "We can get back to poker tonight."

The room stilled as all eyes turned to her. Mia tried to keep her expression casual, but inside she was buzzing. It was perfect—a game that could give her the answers she wanted while offering Rachel a chance to clear the air with Matthew. And of course, it would let Tenner unleash his chaotic streak with dares no sane person would accept.

"All these games, and you want to play truth or dare?" Jon stated ironically, gesturing to the shelves against the wall.

Tenner's eyes lit up with mischief as he leaned forward, abandoning his phone. "Dare," he said, his devilish grin widening.

CHAPTER THIRTY-TWO

Rachel Johnson

NOVEMBER, 2024

"Before we start, let's go over the rules" Mia stood at a corner of the hexagonally shaped table, her voice steady but electric with authority.

The group exchanged wary glances, their curiosity piqued by her sudden confidence. She didn't wait long before continuing, "Rule one: if you don't answer the question or complete the dare, you're out—and you leave the room." She paused, letting the gravity of her words sink in. Tenner's brow raised in mischievous delight, but no one spoke. Satisfied with their hesitant nods, she added, "Rule two: all questions and challenges must be age-appropriate and reasonable."

Mia shot Tenner a warning look, one that only seemed to fuel his excitement. He practically vibrated in his seat with anticipation.

"Alright, Tenner," Matthew said, his grin conspiratorial. "Your dare is to sneak into the great room without being seen and swipe whatever it is your mom is drinking. Bring it back as proof. We'll be watching from the doorway."

The challenge electrified the air. Chairs rolled back quietly as everyone rose to follow Tenner toward the doorway. The group split—Mia and Jon stood to one side, Rachel and Matthew the other. Rachel found herself pressed against the doorframe, Matthew leaning over her shoulder to stay hidden. She froze as his chest brushed against her back, his breath warm against her neck. She prayed he couldn't hear how fast her heart was pounding.

Tenner ducked out into the lobby and crouched low behind the reception desk, his movements exaggerated for effect. He stubbed his toe on the corner, nearly hopping into view before dropping down again with a silent grimace. Rachel felt Matthew stifle a laugh behind her, and she tried to focus on the scene in the great room instead of the tantalizing closeness of him.

Her father sat in the chair Mia usually claimed, arms crossed and sunglasses perched on his face like a barrier against the world. He looked like a toddler in time-out, pouting over some fabricated injustice. Across the room, her mother lounged on the couch, angled away from her sulking husband. The firelight flickered across her features, accentuating the faint droop of her eyelids—a telltale sign of warmth and too many mimosas.

Tenner peeked around the desk and sprinted toward the coat rack by the front door. The bulky mass of scarves and jackets hid him well, but the next leg of his journey was open terrain. Rachel's stomach clenched as he crouched low, preparing to cross the room.

Matthew shifted behind her, and she turned to find him smiling down at her. The look in his eyes sent warmth spiraling through her chest. She realized with a jolt that she had unconsciously pushed her backside into him, and he'd placed a steadying hand on her back. Both felt good. The pressure of his body behind her combined with his controlling touch—it was enough to make her weak in the knees.

Movement in the lobby snapped her attention back to Tenner, who had dropped into an exaggerated army crawl. He slithered across the floor, inching forward with painful precision, each motion so slow it felt agonizing to watch.

Rachel bit her lip to keep from laughing, though her thighs burned from staying crouched in a squat for so long. She could feel Matthew's chest shake lightly with suppressed laughter behind her, his steady presence making her hyper-aware of every small contact between them. She yearned to push back into him and for him to wrap his arms around her and hold her close. The unfamiliar feeling made her dizzy with anticipation. Tenner could take all day to complete his task as far as Rachel was concerned.

Finally, Tenner reached the side table near the couch, where a glass sat, its ice mostly melted. He reached up, plucked it delicately from the surface, and froze. Rachel held her breath, waiting for her mom to stir or her dad to bark out a warning, but neither moved—her mom's eyes now fully closed and her dad with his headphones on and mouth agape. Emboldened, Tenner tipped the glass back, finishing the last watery remnants in one swift gulp.

Rachel slapped a hand over her mouth to stifle a gasp—whether from horror or delight, she wasn't sure. Tenner straightened to his full height and, without so much as a backward glance, strolled out of the great room like he owned the place.

The group scattered back to their seats, stifling their laughter as Tenner triumphantly placed the empty glass on the table. Quiet applause broke out, and he took a bow.

"That was incredible," Matthew said, grinning as he threw Tenner a fist bump.

"What was in there?" Jon asked, sniffing the glass curiously.

"Watered-down Sprite," Tenner replied, laughing. "Guess Dad convinced Mom to take it easy. Explains the sour mood in there."

The tension shifted as Tenner's mischievous grin returned. "Rachel," he said, his eyes gleaming with malice. "Truth or dare?"

Rachel hesitated. She knew better than to accept a dare from Tenner—it would be something humiliating or dangerous. "Truth," she said, bracing herself.

The grin on Tenner's face was wicked. "Have you ever kissed a boy?"

The room went silent. Rachel felt the weight of every gaze on her, her cheeks heating like a furnace. She picked at her nails under the table, her eyes dropping to her lap, wishing she could disappear.

"Eighty million bacteria can be exchanged in one kiss," Mia interrupted smoothly, rescuing her sister with a moment-derailing fact.

"Dang it, Mia!" Tenner groaned, slumping back in his chair.

"I said questions must be age-appropriate," Mia shot back.

Tenner scowled. "She's seventeen!"

"And you're only fourteen, so I'm overruling it." Mia's tone brokered no argument, and Tenner crossed his arms with a pout.

Rachel cast her sister a grateful glance but didn't have time to relax before Mia turned to Matthew, her voice suddenly sharp. "This question is for you."

Her pause was deliberate, building tension as all eyes turned to Matthew. Mia leaned forward, her expression unreadable. Then, with calm reservation, she asked, "Who's the girl in the picture?"

Chapter Thirty-Three

Debbie Atkins

March, 1970

Debbie Atkins woke with a pounding headache.

Darkness pressed against her from all sides—thick, absolute, smothering. She blinked once, twice, then lifted trembling fingers to her face just to make sure her eyes were actually open. They were.

A sharp stab of pain lanced through her temples, so sudden it stole her breath. She clutched her head and froze, afraid to move. If it hadn't already been pitch-black, she might have blacked out from the pain alone.

What the hell happened last night?

Her mind clawed at fragments—music, laughter, someone handing her a red cup, then another. She groaned and massaged her temples, trying to knead memory back into her throbbing skull.

She'd gone to a party. That much she knew. Her friends had begged her to come, promising "just one drink." But the more she thought about it, the less she remembered. And that, more than the headache, terrified her.

This wasn't her. At least not how she was last year.

Back then, life had been simpler—classes, study groups, lesson plans. Debbie had left home two years ago, full of ambition and certainty, to study education at the state's top teaching college. She'd chosen it for its reputation, its structure, its promise of purpose.

But that was before everything changed.

Last year, the school had rebranded itself into a full university, expanding its programs, its population—and its parties. With the new degrees came new faces, mostly men who seemed less interested in academics and more in forming their own "clubs." They weren't fraternities, at least not officially, but the difference was mostly semantic.

Every weekend, they threw enormous, chaotic gatherings—music blaring through dorm walls, the air thick with smoke and cheap beer. They roamed the campus in packs, seeking girls to invite, promising free drinks and "mountain weed" like it was some kind of initiation rite.

Debbie had laughed it off at first. She told herself she could handle it, that she was just having fun. But somewhere along the way, her liver, her lungs, and her GPA had all started keeping score.

And now—here she was.

Lying in the dark, head splitting, not sure where she was... or who might be there with her.

Her thoughts tangled, struggling to make sense of it—had she passed out in some guy's room, or somehow managed to stumble home?

She tried to sit up, but a sick wave of nausea rolled through her. The world tilted, spinning violently, and she dropped back down with a dull thud. Cold. Hard. Wrong.

This wasn't a bed.

Reaching beneath her, her fingers scraped against rough concrete, and when she stretched one arm back, she felt the uneven texture of cinderblocks stacked into an exterior wall. A damp chill seeped through her palms.

Panic fluttered low in her chest.

Slowly, she rolled to her hands and knees and began crawling forward, one cautious movement at a time, her hands sweeping the floor for obstacles. Each breath echoed too loudly in the suffocating dark. She tried to remember the place where they'd been partying—the house, the music, the people—but the memory slipped through her mind like smoke. She'd been too distracted by the boys at the door, all confident smiles and cologne.

She cursed herself now for not paying attention.

Her hand brushed another wall. She turned and began following it, one palm pressed against the base to guide her. The rough surface scraped against her skin.

Then—

Clang!

A bolt of pain exploded through her forehead. She cried out, recoiling. For a few dizzying seconds, white light seemed to burst behind her eyes. *If pain could shine,* she thought deliriously, *I could see the whole damn room right now.*

Groaning, she rubbed her brow with a gritty palm, waiting for the agony to ebb. When it finally dulled to a throb, she reached forward again, determined to find what she'd hit. Her fingers touched something cold and smooth—metal—and then something thinner, rounder.

Her stomach dropped.

Iron bars.

Debbie froze, the chill of realization creeping up her spine. Her fingers tightened around one of the bars. It was thick, solid, unmoving. She rose unsteadily to her feet, pressing her forehead against the cold metal. The bars extended higher than she could reach, spaced evenly—every few inches, another unyielding shaft of iron.

Her breathing quickened.

She shuffled sideways, running her hands along the bars until she met another cinderblock wall. She was boxed in. A cage. A cell.

Her mind reeled. *Was this a basement? A jail? Some kind of sick joke?*

The silence pressed heavier with every heartbeat.

Desperation began to edge out caution. Debbie turned from the bars and groped her way backward, hands outstretched, searching for another wall to confirm the nightmare was complete. Her fingertips brushed cold stone. Trapped.

And then—

A sound behind her.

Scratch.

The unmistakable hiss of a match being struck.

Orange light bloomed against the black, small but blinding after so much darkness.

And in that instant, Debbie knew—she wasn't alone.

Debbie whipped around, her pulse hammering in her ears.

A man stood just beyond the bars, his face illuminated by the flickering flare of a match. He brought the tiny flame to a long, thin taper candle. When the wick caught, the dim orange glow spread outward, licking the concrete walls and casting long, skeletal shadows across the room.

Her breath caught.

She knew that face.

The bartender from the party.

Or at least, that's who she'd thought he was. He'd been older than the rest—late thirties, maybe early forties—standing alone in the kitchen, half in shadow, half in the circle of light above the liquor table. When Debbie had wandered in, tipsy and laughing, he'd smiled politely, asked what she was drinking, and offered to make her something "special."

She'd assumed the guys hosting the party had hired him—some townie paid to pour drinks for college kids.

But now, staring at him through the bars, Debbie's stomach dropped like a stone.

She'd accepted a drink from a stranger.Out of sight from the rest of the party.Next to a back door.

She tried to remember what it had tasted like, what she'd felt after drinking it, but the memory was a fog—blurred edges, missing time. Somewhere between that first sip and waking up in the dark, there was nothing.

He must've drugged her.

Her throat tightened as the realization sank in. *My friends...* Were they looking for her? Had anyone even noticed she was gone? Maybe they thought she'd left with someone. That wouldn't be unusual anymore—not since parties had turned into chaotic free-for-alls, and everyone looked out only for themselves.

The campus used to feel safe. Used to.

Without saying a word, the man crouched, placing the candle carefully on the ground. The flame wavered, throwing his shadow high across the wall. Then he straightened and picked something up from the floor.

A lead pipe.

Debbie's body tensed. Her breath hitched as he stepped toward the bars—one slow, deliberate step at a time. She backed away in rhythm, retreating until her spine pressed against the cold stone.

The iron door creaked open.

The sound was soft, almost delicate, but it sliced through the silence like a scream.

He stepped inside. The candle's light was behind him now, and his face disappeared into shadow. All she could see was the dark shape of his body moving closer, closer still, the pipe glinting faintly in the flicker.

"Please," she whispered, though she wasn't sure if the word even left her throat.

Without warning, the pipe came down.

She threw up her arms instinctively. The blow connected anyway—a brutal crack that sent pain exploding through her skull and shoulders. She collapsed, the world spinning, blood slicking her face and blurring her vision. The metallic tang filled her mouth as she curled in on herself, trembling, trying to protect her head.

A moment later, she heard the hollow clang of metal. The door slamming shut. The scrape of the lock twisting back into place.

Then silence.

Debbie lifted her head with effort. The candle still flickered, guttering low, but the man was gone. Through her swimming vision, she caught only a shadow shifting at the edge of the light—then, the sound of a deep breath.

And darkness swallowed everything again.

He'd blown out the candle.

Her heart thundered in her chest as she lay there, blood cooling on her skin. He was toying with her—testing her fear, stretching it out like wire.

And worse, she realized with a dawning horror—no one knew she was missing.

No one was coming.

How long could she survive this?

CHAPTER THIRTY-FOUR

Mia Johnson

NOVEMBER, 2024

The chandelier above the poker table flickered, casting jagged shadows across the room as a thick cloud swallowed the sun. The once vibrant game room turned somber, its warmth drained in an instant. The weight in the air was palpable, pressing on the group like a silent accusation.

All eyes locked onto Mia. Everyone except Jon, who exchanged a look with Matthew—one that spoke volumes of shared pain and unspoken understanding. Matthew's gaze bore into Mia, unflinching and intense. She held her ground, her expression steady despite the unease pooling in her chest. She knew the truth—or at least a fragment of it—but she needed more. She wasn't asking out of idle curiosity. The girl was unlike any spirit Mia had ever seen. Other sightings were more like blurred shapes or movements caught out of the corner of her eye. This girl was different. Mia had seen her, flesh and bone—or what looked like it. If it hadn't been for that encounter, this would feel unforgivably intrusive.

Matthew drew a sharp breath, ready to speak, but Jon interrupted. "Stop. You don't have to answer that."

Matthew raised a hand to silence him, his jaw tight. "No. It's okay." His voice was gravelly, as though forcing the words through a sieve of buried emotion. "We've avoided talking about her for far too long. Maybe it's time we stop running away from her memory."

Tenner and Rachel leaned forward, their brows furrowed in confusion. Mia's question seemed to fester like an open wound. They didn't know who this girl was or how Mia had even known to ask, but the tension said everything: this wasn't family lore. This was pain, raw and unresolved.

Matthew tapped at his phone, pulling up the photo from his lock screen and sliding it to the center of the table. The screen illuminated a young girl with striking black hair and deep, curious eyes. Her smile was radiant, full of hope, but it didn't match the haunted teen Mia had glimpsed in the lobby. In the photo, she was still a child, untouched by whatever had stolen that brightness.

"That's Ana," Matthew said, his voice trembling. "Our sister."

Mia's heart skipped. Did they not know? He spoke of her in the present tense, not past—a subtle rebellion against the truth they all seemed unwilling to confront.

"When Dad got sick, we each coped in our own way," Matthew began, his words slow and deliberate. "Jon hit the gym like it was a religion. Manny locked himself in his room. I buried myself in school, trying to stay numb. But Ana... she lashed out. It started with little things—snapping at us, slamming doors. Then it got worse. She started blaming Mom for every-thing. Every fight between them was like watching a storm tear through the house. Dad bought her a journal, hoping she'd pour her feelings into something constructive, but it only made her angrier."

He paused, dragging a hand down his face as if the memory itself was exhausting. "When Dad passed, Ana exploded. She became someone none of us recognized. One night, everything boiled over. She accused Mom of things I still can't believe. It turned physical. She attacked her. Knocked her down in the kitchen. Mom hit her head on the counter and just sat there, bleeding... refusing to fight back."

Matthew's voice cracked, and his hands clenched into fists. "Ana ran out that night. She left. And we haven't seen or heard from her since."

Mia fought against the urge to gasp and kept her gaze steady.

"Did you try to find her?" Tenner's voice was barely above a whisper, the innocence in his question like salt in an open wound.

Jon nodded solemnly. "We searched everywhere. Called every friend she had, knocked on every door. We even combed through the woods she loved so much. It was her safe place. Or... it used to be." His voice faltered, and he looked away, his cheeks reddening. "I don't think she wants to be found."

The silence that followed was suffocating, each of them sinking under the weight of grief that was both fresh and ancient. Then a voice from the doorway broke the stillness.

"Mom won't let us talk about her. Not that it helps. She suffers every day—the not knowing. She has no closure. None of us do."

Manny stood leaning against the doorframe like it was the only thing keeping him upright. His face was unreadable, but his voice carried the same burden as his brothers'. "Mom tried everything to help Ana through her pain, but she still blames herself. She's never stopped blaming herself."

The brothers exchanged a look, a silent communion of shared guilt and love. Manny straightened, his gaze softening enough to betray the sadness beneath. "We just... hope she's happy. Somewhere."

Mia swallowed hard, guilt twisting her stomach into knots. She felt the room spinning around her as she discovered the gravity of her question. She shouldn't have asked—not like this. Not when the truth she carried weighed heavier than anything they had revealed. She knew where Ana was, and it was *not* a happy place. Not even close.

Rachel wiped a tear from her cheek, her fingers trembling as she tried to compose herself averting her gaze to the playing cards and lead pipe game piece on the bookshelf. She looked ready to throw her arms around Matthew but held back, her restraint only adding to the charged atmosphere. Tenner sat stiffly, his wide eyes bouncing between his siblings and Manny, as if seeing him for the first time.

Mia glanced at Manny. Was his strange demeanor a result of this trauma? Were these cracks in their family—their guilt, their grief—why he seemed so disconnected from the world? She didn't know. What she did know was that the truth would shatter them, and maybe, just maybe, ignorance was a mercy they didn't even know they needed.

CHAPTER THIRTY-FIVE

Rachel Johnson

NOVEMBER, 2024

Mia shot to her feet, the sudden motion snapping everyone's attention to her. She tore her gaze from Manny, who still lingered awkwardly in the doorway, and glanced sharply at the others seated around the table.

"Dare," she said firmly, her change of subject sudden. Mia was always the first to offer herself up, the one who stepped into the line of fire to shift an atmosphere that had grown too heavy. The weight in the room seemed to ease, if only slightly.

Rachel glanced at Tenner, catching the way he shifted eagerly in his seat, clearly racking his brain for a challenge—something edgy but still acceptable. But as Rachel turned her eyes back toward Mia, her gaze drifted beyond her sister, out through the front windows, and her breath caught.

"Oh my gosh," she murmured, her voice barely audible over the hum of the room.

All eyes followed hers to the window. Chairs rolled against the floor as the group stood in near unison, craning to see outside. Even Manny, hesitant and unsure, stepped into the room for a better view.

Outside, a blanket of snow covered the driveway, pristine and shimmering under the glow of the flickering porch light. The trees stood heavy with the weight of it, their branches drooping under thick, fluffy pillows of white. The snowfall had crept in undiscovered, silencing the world beyond the glass. Now it came down with a fierce intensity, swirling in chaotic flurries and reducing visibility. The lights flickered again, adding a sense of foreboding, casting the scene in a dim glow.

"Hey, kids," came a quiet, familiar voice from the doorway.

Rachel turned to find her mother standing there, leaning heavily against the frame. She looked exhausted, her hair disheveled and her face drawn, but her voice carried the same soft authority it always had.

"Oh, it's snowing," her mom murmured, her brow furrowing in mild confusion. "How did I miss that?"

Rachel's lips pressed into a thin line. She knew exactly how her mother had missed it. She'd been passed out on the couch again, worn down by the stress of her job and the relentless demands of their father's care—and, of course, the copious amounts of alcohol.

Her mother's eyes lingered on the snow for a moment, but her gaze seemed distant, as though her thoughts were far from the winter storm.

"Mom?" Rachel prompted gently, concern lacing her voice.

She blinked and shifted her focus to Rachel, her tired eyes attempting a flicker of warmth. A faint smile teased at the corner of her lips but failed to reach the rest of her face. "I'm taking your dad upstairs to rest," she said, her tone flat and matter-of-fact. "His headache is getting worse."

Her expression darkened for a brief moment, an edge of frustration slipping through the fatigue. Rachel didn't blame her. Her dad's headaches were unbearable for everyone, but no one bore the brunt of them more than her dedicated mother. Not even their dad. The guilt gnawed at Rachel every time, knowing how much her mom sacrificed for a man who, most days, was more burden than partner. She wondered—not for the first time—if her mom regretted staying. Once, he'd been a star football player, the picture of strength and success. Now, he was an injured shell of that man, unable to hold a job and constantly dependent on her care.

Rachel watched as her mom wrapped a supportive arm around David's waist, guiding him with practiced care toward the stairs. The quiet creak of their footsteps faded as they ascended. Rachel sighed, her focus shifting back to the others—until she heard Mia's sharp intake of breath.

"Mia?" Tenner asked, his tone cautious as he followed her wide-eyed gaze toward the doorway.

Mia stood frozen, her face ghostly pale, even for her. Her hands were clenched into tight fists at her sides, and her chest rose and fell in shallow, uneven breaths.

"What?" Tenner pressed again, louder this time.

Mia blinked rapidly, snapping herself out of the trance, but her voice, when it came, was jagged and rushed. "The dead outnumber the living fifteen to one," she blurted out, the words tumbling from her lips like an incantation. Looking around for a reaction, all she received was silence. Heavy and charged.

Matthew broke it first, a chuckle escaping as he tried to lighten the mood. "We better go see if Mom needs help. This snow could throw a wrench in things," he said.

With one last glance at the swirling snow storm outside, Matthew and his brothers shuffled out of the room, their retreat leaving an oppressive stillness in their wake. Rachel's stomach twisted as she watched them go, longing for the moment before their playful game had turned so ominous, before Mia's eerie question had left them all shaken.

But there was no going back now.

Chapter Thirty-Six

Mia Johnson

November, 2024

Mia spent most of the day in the game room, perched on the wide window seat with her legs tucked beneath her, watching the relentless snowfall blur the world outside. Tenner sat at the nearby table, painstakingly stacking cards into a precarious tower. The room was quiet except for the occasional flutter of cards collapsing and Tenner's mumbled curses.

The lodge's spotty internet signal had vanished entirely, leaving them cut off from the outside world. Rachel was holed up in her room working on her essay, their parents were napping, and Mia had taken it upon herself to keep an eye on Tenner. She couldn't trust him not to attempt something ridiculous—like surfing the stairs on a mattress—and with a blizzard raging outside, a broken leg would spell disaster. Emergency vehicles, no matter how well-equipped, wouldn't be able to navigate the snow-covered mountain roads.

Still, Mia's thoughts weren't on Tenner for long. They kept circling back to Ana. Matthew's story had left too many questions unanswered. Ana had clearly intended to run away, but what had happened next? How had she ended up in this old mountain lodge? Had she hidden here? If so, how had she died, and why hadn't she sought help? And if Ana had died in the lodge, as her wandering ghost implied, why hadn't anyone found her body during the renovation?

Mia frowned, her forehead pressing against the cold glass. That kind of discovery didn't just get overlooked, did it? She imagined the scandal if the press found out a dead body had been unearthed in a newly renovated lodge. That alone could doom a new business. Had someone swept it under the rug to avoid bad publicity?

A memory flashed through her mind—of their drive up the mountain, stopping at a quaint little shop in the valley. By the register, a depressing bulletin board had caught her eye. It had been plastered with missing posters, not one or two but dozens. Black-and-white photos of people who had vanished without a trace, their faces frozen in time, surrounded by tiny tear-off tabs with contact numbers dangling below. Was there a poster for Ana hidden below them? Had her brothers created one while searching for her? The thought sent a shiver down Mia's spine, bringing her back to the haunted look on Ana's face as she appeared at the base of the stairs where only moments before Lisa and David stood.

The flutter of falling cards pulled her back to the present, followed by Tenner's quiet curse. He'd been at it for hours, stubbornly determined to build a card tower, though it had collapsed more times than she could count.

"Let's head into the great room," Mia suggested, pushing herself off the windowsill. "It's getting cold in here, and dinner should be ready soon."

Tenner shoved the playing cards off the table in frustration, but as Mia moved toward the door, she heard him sigh and bend down to pick them up. He was slow to follow, but she didn't wait.

As she passed the reception area, she spotted Jon setting up a cot in the office. He glanced up and gave her a wary smile before returning to his task. Mia offered him a small nod and kept walking, her thoughts still scattered. Was he angry she had so carelessly brought up their families private past, asking the question they had been avoiding for years?

"Mia, dear," Valentina called as she emerged gracefully from the kitchen, wiping her hands on her apron. "Come take a seat. Dinner will be ready shortly."

Mia was heading for her usual chair but changed course, plopping onto one of the benches at the long dining table instead. "Oh," Valentina continued, her voice less cheerful, "I spoke with your mom. Your dad isn't feeling well, so they'll be taking their dinner upstairs."

As Jon crossed the room toward the kitchen, Mia rolled her eyes, wondering how much of her parents' retreat upstairs was due to her dad's headache—and how much was an excuse to duck out of conversation and lose himself in a podcast. Once he started a new episode, he had a hard time pulling away until it was finished.

Surely this vacation was throwing a wrench in his listening schedule.

Leave it to her mom to plan a *"family getaway"* only to drink herself into oblivion and leave the kids in the care of the chef—who already had three children of her own.

Well, *four*, technically.

Mia leaned back against the wall, her eyes drifting once again to the window.

Snow continued to fall in heavy, swirling sheets, more than she'd ever seen in her life. Growing up in southeastern North Carolina, snow was a rare novelty, but this storm felt oppressive as if the weight of the snow would cave the old lodge in, burying them in an icy tomb.

Tenner slid onto the bench across from her, and Mia noted Valentina was still standing at her side. She wasn't looking at Mia but out the window, her expression unusually somber. For the first time, Mia saw the ever-cheerful woman as vulnerable, weighed down by something unspoken. Did she imagine her daughter out in the treacherous storm?

"Are you staying tonight?" Mia asked, already knowing the answer but feeling the need to fill the silence.

"Yes," Valentina replied softly. "I spoke with your mother. I had planned to have the boys sleep in the office. We have fold away cots in addition to the bed that's already in there. I was going to take the couch, but your mother insisted I stay in Rachel's room. Rachel will move into yours until the storm passes. I hope you don't mind."

Valentina's voice faltered, and she bowed her head, staring at the floor. The shift in her demeanor tugged at Mia's heart in an unfamiliar way.

"It's fine," Mia said gently, though the thought of sharing a room with Rachel again made her start to sweat. At least they would have two beds this time. "We probably shouldn't have taken up two rooms to begin with."

Rachel appeared then, rounding the corner and flopping onto the bench beside Mia. "Hey, roomie," Mia said, offering a fist bump. Rachel ignored her, instead shooting a sympathetic glance at Valentina's retreating figure.

"Control your face," Mia hissed under her breath.

Rachel blinked at her, confused. "What?"

"She doesn't know that we know about…," Mia's whisper trailed off, leaning closer. "All she knows is that she had to kick you out of your room because of the storm. Don't make it weird."

Rachel's expression contorted into something between a grimace and a smirk. Mia couldn't tell if it was supposed to be an apology or defiance, but it was better than pity.

Matthew, Jon, and Manny emerged from the kitchen carrying platters of food—burgers, grilled chicken, buns, and salad. Valentina followed with a caddy of condiments, her usual cheer returning as if the kitchen door was her reset button. She directed her boys to sit.

"You're off duty now," she said firmly to her boys as they hesitantly took their seats. "Relax and eat. You're guests tonight."

Jon opened his mouth to protest, but Valentina silenced him with a single look.

Despite the food in front of them, no one moved. The six teens sat in silence, tension thick in the air, until Matthew and Jon spoke in unison: "Eat."

Manny rolled his eyes, tossing a burger onto his plate, and muttered, "If only Murdoch could see us now."

Manny grunted as Matthew's foot kicked his shin under the table, though the look on his face was more of a threat than the kick itself. Mia finally reached for a plate. But even as they began to eat, she couldn't shake the unease that had surrounded the group with their new shared secrets.

CHAPTER THIRTY-SEVEN

Rachel Johnson

NOVEMBER, 2024

Rachel chewed at the edges of her burger with careful precision, nibbling small bites as though it were an art form. She didn't want to seem like a glutton, but more importantly, she wanted to avoid an embarrassing moment if Matthew directed a question her way while she was mid-chew. To offset her slow eating, she drank water in frequent, regular intervals, as if the blizzard outside had become an arid desert.

"So," she began, her tone light, testing the waters for a casual conversation. "Am I the only one who hears the house moaning at night?"

Her attempt at humor landed with an audible thud. The atmosphere at the table shifted, and as Rachel scanned the faces around her, it became clear she wasn't alone in her observation.

"When a person dies, their sense of hearing is the last to go," Mia chimed in.

Tenner broke the silence following Mia's morbid factoid, his voice muffled as he spoke around a bite of his towering double cheeseburger. "Probably some animal in the woods," he said, brushing it off. "I've heard it too."

"It's not coming from the woods," Mia said firmly, her face devoid of humor.

Rachel turned to her sister, surprised. "Yeah, it's the house. It's old, right?— bound to make some strange noises."

The three brothers exchanged a glance, a silent conversation passing between them, and Mia called them out. "You know it's coming from inside the house, don't you?" she pressed.

Small goosebumps rose on Rachel's arms noting the slight differences between Mia's reference to a sound coming from inside the house in contrast to Rachel's own comments about the odd noises coming from the house itself. Any well-built structure shifts with the land, as it settles with time or changes with the seasons and accompanying temperature fluctuations. But to imply that a sound was coming from inside the house infers it is coming from *something* inside rather than the structure itself.

To Rachel's surprise, it was Manny who answered. "There's nothing in the house," he said, but his words lacked conviction. His eyes darted between his brothers before he added, "But there is... something. We've all heard it, but we've checked. There's no dying animal in the walls or busted water heater groaning at night." Manny's eyes fell to his half-eaten burger. "We don't know what it is."

Mia leaned forward, her voice lowering as she challenged him. "So you admit it's something?"

Jon, who had been silent until now, cut in with an edge to his tone. "Look, we're on top of a mountain, surrounded by woods, staying in a house that's pushing a hundred years old. Of course, there are going to be noises—unsettling ones, even. But that's not a reason to do anything reckless. It's why we should stay in our rooms at night."

Rachel exhaled, her shoulders relaxing once more with Jon's rational argument.

Mia's eyes narrowed, her sharp instincts catching the slip. "If it's just the house, why does it matter if we leave our rooms?"

Jon hesitated for the briefest moment before correcting himself. "I meant the lodge. We should stay inside the lodge. There's no telling what's out there in the storm."

Rachel glanced between Mia and Jon, the tension between them as palpable as the cold draft creeping under the doors. Mia seemed determined to dig at something, some truth Jon clearly didn't want to reveal. The dynamic unnerved Rachel, though she wasn't sure why. She was curious—more than curious—but she would never pry like Mia. What led Rachel to her academic achievements was the relentless desire for information. She was always eager to learn more, to find the answer to *Why?* Rachel valued answers, sure, but she valued boundaries, too. Mia had no such qualms.

The conversation died as quickly as it had started. Plates began to empty, and the rhythmic clatter of silverware signaled the end of the meal. The boys began to clear the table, but the noise drew Valentina from the kitchen. She clapped her hands sharply. "No, no, no. That's enough from you boys for today. Go set up in the office. I'll handle this."

Matthew hesitated, a plate in his hand, before setting it down. Turning to Rachel, he extended his hand toward her.

For a moment, Rachel blinked at him, confused. Was he asking for her plate? Mia's exasperated scoff and Tenner's quiet laugh clued her in. He was offering to help her up.

Her cheeks burned as she placed her hand in his, any previous concerns about the house, the woods, the sounds... gone. Matthew's grip was firm yet gentle, his hand surprisingly soft for someone who spent so much time working around the lodge. Rachel's heart fluttered with an inexplicable urge—to squeeze his hand, to kiss it, or even to bite the fleshy part below his thumb. She gave her head a subtle shake, trying to banish the ridiculous, even slightly devious thought.

Matthew led her toward the stairs, his hand still holding hers. When they reached the base, he stopped and turned to face her. His hazel eyes caught the light, and for a split second, Rachel thought he might lean in. Her thoughts raced—were her lips chapped? Did she smell like a cheeseburger?

But instead of the kiss she half-expected, his voice broke through her spiraling thoughts. "Promise me you'll stay in your room tonight," he said, his tone serious.

Rachel blinked, thrown off balance, her stomach dropping once again. "What?"

"After you get ready for bed, lock the door and don't come out until morning," he said, his eyes locked onto hers. "Please."

There was a weight to his words, a gravity that sent a chill crawling up her spine. Unsure of how to respond, she nodded. "Okay," she whispered.

Matthew raised her hand, his full lips brushing softly against the back of it. His gaze never wavered from hers. "Goodnight," he said, his voice low, almost a whisper.

He released her hand and turned away, leaving Rachel standing there, her heart pounding in her chest as she watched him walk toward the office.

CHAPTER THIRTY-EIGHT

Mia Johnson

NOVEMBER, 2024

The thought of venturing out in the dark, even for the tempting closeness of Matthew, hadn't been enough to get Rachel to brush her teeth before bed.

"Just skip tonight," Rachel had urged, her voice small and shaky.

"That's really gross," Mia had replied, already reaching for the door.

"But we need to lock the door," Rachel pressed, her wide eyes peeking over the twin covers pulled up to her chin. She looked fragile, like a child who was afraid of monsters under the bed.

"I'll lock it when I come back," Mia had reassured her, but Rachel's fearful expression lingered in her mind as she stepped into the hall. "You can scream if you need me, you know. Loudly. I'll be right in the bathroom," she added, pausing to meet her sister's gaze, "brushing my teeth."

When she returned, the room was eerily quiet. To her surprise, Rachel had managed to fall asleep despite her nerves. Mia, however, wasn't so lucky. She locked the door but couldn't stop the flood of unanswered questions. Why were the boys so insistent on them staying in their rooms? If they weren't telling the whole truth, it meant there was something serious to fear.

She couldn't shake the memory of the hidden compartment under her bed, its presence an undeniable clue that the house harbored secrets. Tomorrow, she decided, she'd search again. Tonight, though, she didn't dare risk waking Rachel. The last thing she needed was her nervous and scared sister awake to put her further on edge.

It felt like she'd only just closed her eyes when a distant slam jolted her awake.

Mia threw the covers off and sat up, her heart hammering. She glanced over at Rachel, but her sister slept soundly. It wasn't the familiar groaning of the old lodge—it was sharper, more deliberate. As she swung her legs out of bed, her gaze caught movement outside the frosted window.

She hesitated. It was probably snow falling from a branch, she told herself. Still, the unease creeping up her spine wouldn't let her ignore it. She leaned across the nightstand and pressed her face to the cold glass.

Her breath hitched. It wasn't a branch.

A figure bundled in snow gear trudged across the yard, its movements purposeful. What made her blood run cold was the large blanketed bundle they carried—limp and heavy, over their shoulder.

Goosebumps rose on her skin. She rubbed at the frost on the windowpane with her sleeve, trying to see more clearly. When she cleared away most of the foggy obstruction, she looked again. The figure turned sharply, and their gaze locked onto hers.

The mysterious figure's face was obscured except for a slit that revealed piercing eyes, but the intent was unmistakable. They knew she was there. They were watching for her.

Mia ducked instinctively, hitting her head on the edge of the nightstand as she dropped to the floor. Pain radiated across her skull, but she barely noticed it over the pounding of her heart.

Rachel was somehow still asleep, curled up tightly in her bed, oblivious to the threat outside. But what about the others?

Throwing caution aside, Mia unlocked the door and bolted into the hallway. She flung open Tenner's door—relief washing over her when she found him safe and asleep.

She gripped the balcony rail for balance, gasping for breath before turning to check her parents' room. A banging noise from downstairs pulled her attention and her eyes to the first floor. She whirled around and sprinted down the stairs, nearly colliding with Matthew at the bottom.

"What's going on?" he asked, his voice thick with sleep.

"A man!" Mia gasped. "Outside! He was carrying... " She broke off, the words catching in her throat. "I think it was a body."

Matthew's brows knitted together, his concern tempered with skepticism. "Mia, it sounds like you had a bad dream. This house can do that to people."

Behind him, Manny appeared, his voice, quiet as a whisper. "Mom?"

His usual stoicism cracked, revealing sheer horror in his expression. The sight of him—so unnerved—was enough to jolt Matthew fully awake. Without another word, Matthew turned and bolted up the stairs.

Valentina stepped out of Rachel's room as he reached the top. Matthew folded her into a tight embrace, his shoulders trembling as he whispered something in Spanish Mia couldn't make out.

Valentina turned to the rest of the group, her gaze sharp and probing. "What is going on out here?" she demanded, propping her hands upon her hips, sounding less like the composed hostess Mia knew and more like a fiercely protective mother.

Jon rounded the stairs from the great room, his voice steady but rehearsed. "Mia had a nightmare. We're taking care of it. Everything's fine."

Valentina's eyes lingered on each of them, her doubt evident, but after a long pause, she nodded and retreated into the room, closing the door firmly behind her.

Mia stared at Jon, taking in his sudden appearance and flushed cheeks. "Where did you come from?"

Jon placed his hands firmly on her shoulders. "Listen to me," he said, his tone condescending and cold. "I know you think you saw something, but everyone is safe. Go back to bed, lock your door, and in the morning, this will all seem like a bad dream."

His words were calm, but the look in his eyes betrayed him. He didn't believe a word he'd said.

Mia stared back at him, her stomach churning with frustration and fear. She climbed the stairs without another word, her resolve hardening with each step. When she reached the top, she turned around to find all three boys standing at the base, arms crossed, and watching her intently. Rolling her eyes, Mia feigned confidence that was waning with each moment. It wasn't until she closed and locked her door that she was able to let out her held breath.

The figure, the body—or whatever it was—would have to wait until morning. But she swore to herself: tomorrow, she would find answers.

CHAPTER THIRTY-NINE

Ella Whitmore

OCTOBER, 2024

The town of Maple Ridge was as picturesque as a postcard. The narrow street was flanked by cafés, boutiques, and art galleries. Planters overflowing with fall foliage hung from the stylish lampposts. Young moms in leggings and cropped hoodies pushed strollers while sipping warm, seasonal drinks. Store owners propped up A-frame chalkboards and mounted flags as they opened for the day. The maple trees lining the sidewalks were a deep, burning red and had begun to shed their leaves, dotting the pale concrete like confetti.

Ella parked her car and strolled down the street, feeling invigorated by the crisp mountain air. Beyond the main stretch of shops, she came upon a gingerbread-style bungalow with a wooden sign swinging gently in the breeze: Meemaw's B&B.

She'd already learned there were no hotel chains in the valley, but had hoped to find something local to avoid the long drive back to Boone. This would do.

Meemaw was old. *Very* old. Ella couldn't guess her age—either she was a relic from another century, or life had been extraordinarily unkind. Her face was wrinkled like a Shar Pei, and the tremors in her hands made the loose skin on her arms ripple with each movement. Her gray hair was pulled into a loose bun, and her eyes were so clouded it was a wonder she could see at all.

Still, after confirming a vacancy, Ella moved her car and checked in.

What was supposed to be a quick power nap turned into a four-hour sleep. The mountain air and the soft village sounds drifting through the open window had lulled her under fast and deep.

She freshened up quickly and jogged down the stairs—only to find Meemaw waiting at the bottom, holding a bagged lunch.

"I heard you wake. Floors are thin," Meemaw offered by way of explanation. "Anyway, I reckoned you needed something to eat. Maybe I should rename this place Meemaw's B&L."

Ella thanked her as the old woman turned and shuffled away, chuckling at her own joke.

"Oh—bed and lunch. I get it," Ella said with a smile, embarrassed that the punchline had almost gone over her head. "Actually, can I ask you a question?"

Meemaw paused but didn't turn fully around. Even the smallest movement seemed like a chore. "Yes, dear. Anything you need."

"Do you know anything about an old mountain lodge that was around here in the late 1900s, called The Hilltop Escape?"

Meemaw's jaw dropped. She froze where she stood—her tremors vanishing so suddenly it was as if time had stopped.

Ella stared, half expecting the woman to keel over right there on the floor. She took a cautious step forward.

Then Meemaw's expression shifted—from shock to something darker. Anger.

Without a word, she raised one shaky hand and pointed to the door with force that belied her age. "Go!" she barked.

Ella stood frozen for a beat, stunned, then dropped her bagged lunch and stumbled toward the door. She stepped out onto the porch, heart thudding, and tried to process what had just happened.

As she reached the sidewalk, still reeling, she heard the sharp click of the deadbolt sliding into place behind her.

The street suddenly seemed far less cheerful than it had that morning. The sidewalks were empty, the flags hung limp against the storefronts, and the once-vibrant maple trees now looked strangely ominous in the shifting light. It wasn't until she reached the far end of Main Street that Ella ascertained why.

The sun had dipped behind the towering mountain above the town, casting everything below into a shadow.

She pushed through the door of a café, bumping a little bell suspended from the ceiling—its tinny jingle announcing her arrival. The man behind the counter looked up from a mystery novel and smiled.

Ella returned the smile, noting that the only other person in the café was a twenty-something guy wiping down tables near the back.

"Take a seat," the man behind the counter called, before turning to his co-worker. "You got this, Josh? I'm gonna run to the bank while it's slow."

The guy wiping tables—Josh, presumably—nodded, grabbed a menu, and headed toward Ella, who had settled by the window.

"We don't get many people in here this time of day," he said with a friendly smile.

"Why not?" Ella asked, genuinely puzzled, taking a quick glance at her watch. "It's just after noon."

"We're slammed in the mornings when the sun's out, and again in the evenings once it's dark. But no one around here really comes out during the afternoon—not when we're in the shadow."

Ella straightened in her seat. There was something in his tone. Something that made her feel like she was on the edge of understanding—like a page was about to turn.

She leaned forward slightly, lowering her voice. "Do you know anything about a place called the *Hilltop Escape*?"

Josh froze—not with fear like Meemaw, but with surprise. He glanced quickly over his shoulder, watching as his coworker disappeared into the back room.

"Give me a minute, okay?" he whispered. Then, raising his voice, added casually, "What can I get you to drink?"

CHAPTER FORTY

Rachel Johnson

NOVEMBER, 2024

Rachel stumbled groggily out of Mia's bedroom, her head foggy from sleep. The dim light of the early morning seeped through the cracks in the lodge's heavy curtains, casting long shadows across the hall. She froze in place when she saw her dad standing outside his open door. He wasn't moving, only staring intently toward the balcony as though something invisible held his gaze. Slowly, he turned his head toward her, his face a mask of exhaustion, his eyes hollow and distant. He looked at her—or perhaps through her—before retreating back into his room and quietly shutting the door. The click of the latch felt unnervingly final.

A faint murmur of voices drifted up from the great room below. Rachel immediately recognized her mother's tone, sharp yet low, attempting to keep her voice hushed despite the lodge's open layout betraying her. The acoustics carried every word to the upper levels. Intrigued, Rachel tiptoed past her parents' room, careful not to creak the floorboards, and crouched near the far end of the balcony. Pressing her back to the wall, she positioned herself to eavesdrop, peeking through the wooden slats of the railing.

From her bird's eye view, Rachel spotted her mom on the sofa below. Instead of the vacation staple of a mimosa, she was nursing a coffee, the steam curling in the crisp air. In a chair across from her, Valentina sat stiffly—her expression carefully neutral.

"I knew early on that I was signing up to be a caregiver for what is essentially four children," her mom said bitterly, her voice laced with frustration. "But a little appreciation wouldn't hurt. It's like he's two different people. Around the kids, he's Mr. Perfect Dad. But when we're alone, he's constantly criticizing me—my cooking, my cleaning, everything. And now this whole vacation is ruined because *my* drink triggered one of his headaches."

Valentina shifted slightly, and Rachel couldn't tell if it was out of awkwardness from the personal one-sided conversation or the lingering discomfort of spending the night in an unfamiliar bed. Whatever the reason, her mother didn't seem to notice. It must be hard to listen to someone complain about caring for a spouse with occasional headaches when you watched your husband die and daughter disappear.

"Yesterday, I brought him dinner—placed it right in front of him—and instead of thanking me, he waved me off and snapped at me for interrupting his stupid podcast. Honestly, who listens to *that* much true crime? It's disturbing. He's either asleep, knocked out from his meds, or in his own little world of crime and punishment."

Valentina opened her mouth to speak, but Rachel's mother didn't pause long enough to give her the chance. "And get this," she said, her voice dropping conspiratorially, "when he renewed our insurance policy this year, he made changes, increasing the payout. Not just to my life insurance, but to the kids' too."

Rachel's stomach twisted and she instinctively looked back to the door of her parent's bedroom. She sat up straighter, straining to hear every word. Below her, Valentina's expression shifted from polite discomfort to genuine concern. "Maybe it was a mistake?" Valentina suggested carefully, leaning forward. "Those forms can be confusing. And the benefits seem to change every year."

The explanation was reasonable, logical even, but it did little to calm the knot of anxiety tightening in Rachel's chest. Could her dad really have changed their policies intentionally? She shook the thought away. Her dad wasn't perfect, but he'd always been devoted to his family. His life revolved around them. He didn't work, didn't have friends or hobbies, but he was always there for them whether it be family movie night or helping with a school project. It had to be a misunderstanding. His life revolved around his family—and the true crime podcasts.

Her thoughts were interrupted by the sudden creak of a door. Across the hall, Tenner's bedroom door swung open. Startled, Rachel jumped, accidentally bumping the balcony railing with a loud *thunk*. She felt like a criminal caught in the act.

Tenner groaned, rubbing his eyes as he stared at her crouched form. "Seriously, Rachel? This is getting weird." He shook his head and shuffled toward the bathroom before she could explain herself.

The sounds of the door and their brief exchange must have carried down to the great room because her mom stiffened, pulling her robe tightly around her. The moment of vulnerability evaporated as she stood abruptly, her tone now at a normal level yet tinged with guilt. "I'd better take some breakfast up to David," she mumbled, avoiding Valentina's gaze.

Rachel rose from her hiding spot, realizing there was no point in spying anymore. Her hand on the solid, ornate balcony railing felt as cold as ice and she pulled it back defensively. She descended the stairs slowly, passing her mom on the way. She balanced a tray with a bowl of oatmeal, a glass of water, and a cup of coffee. Rachel smiled faintly, trying to mask the growing unease in her chest, but said nothing.

Her mom had been keeping so much bottled up—her frustrations, her doubts. If she was hiding this, what else didn't Rachel know?

CHAPTER FORTY-ONE

Merion Stroll

JANUARY, 1973

Merion stood at the balcony enjoying the view into the great room below—the early morning sunshine carrying joyful light and warmth through the frosted windows. She was excited to have a solo vacation. So what if her friend bailed on her. She could have just as much fun exploring the mountains on her own.

Ready to take on the day, Merion reached both arms up to the sky and stretched—raising up on her tippy-toes—when a powerful push from behind flung her over the solid, ornate balcony. She landed without grace, limbs splayed at grotesque, unnatural positions, on the long wooden table below.

Chapter Forty-Two

Mia Johnson

November, 2024

The sun was barely up, but produced enough light for Mia to see out her bedroom window and into the woods. The path showed little signs of use, just a narrow opening of cleared branches, leaves, and other natural debris. Even when they'd walked the path there were times the direction was unclear and they depended on Matthew and Jon to lead the way. Either the lodge has not attracted enough business yet or their visitors haven't been big hikers. One would think the beautiful mountaintop would attract outdoor enthusiasts from the village regularly, but the area seemed to be a local taboo.

A strange sensation crawled up the back of her neck before it hit her. Gone were the frosted window panes, and there wasn't a snowflake to be seen. The ground which had been covered with ice and snow and the storm showing no sign of stopping was now brown with a combination of turned leaves and mud.

Mia pulled her line of sight back from the woods outside to take in the outline of her reflection in the window, when a secondary reflection appeared next to hers.

Mia whipped around and found herself face to face with Ana. Not the haunted Ana she'd seen in the window or the sad Ana who lingered behind Jon, but the Ana from the photo on Matthew's phone.

The longer she stared, the wider her eyes grew. Her kind, youthful face distorted as her eyes contorted and grew to half the size of her face. When her mouth slowly opened, Mia nearly expected roaches to crawl out but instead, she uttered one chilling word, "MURDER!"

CHAPTER FORTY-THREE

Mia Johnson

NOVEMBER, 2024

Mia woke with a jolt, her heart pounding in her chest and cold sweat causing the cheap sheets to rip from her back like velcro. She blinked, disoriented, the edges of her nightmare clinging to her like cobwebs. Hours of tossing and turning had convinced her sleep wouldn't come, yet here she was, startled awake from what had apparently been a deep slumber. She sat up, her pulse quickening when she noticed Rachel's bed was empty.

Her first thought sent panic surging through her veins—*Where's Rachel?* But then her gaze shifted, and she observed the bed was not only empty but neatly made. A shaky laugh escaped her lips as she slumped back against her own pillow. *Kidnappers don't make the bed after taking their victims,* she thought dryly, the absurdity of her imagination not fully dispelling her lingering unease. Neither do ghosts.

Throwing the covers aside, Mia padded over to the window. The icy chill of the glass seeped through her fingertips as she pressed her hands against it, gazing out into the snowy expanse beyond the lodge. The unease from the night before bubbled back to the surface.

Had she really seen someone out there? A figure moving through the snow, carrying what looked like a limp body slung over their shoulder? She'd convinced herself at the time that something evil was taking place. But now, in the stark clarity of daylight, she wasn't so sure. Everyone in the house was accounted for—she had checked, right? And there wasn't another living soul around for miles.

Still, the memory of that figure, the slow, deliberate way it had moved, made her stomach twist. Mia's breath fogged the window as she leaned closer, scanning the untouched blanket of snow below. As she expected, there was nothing. No footprints. No drag marks. No evidence that anything—or anyone—had crossed from the house to the tree line.

Sighing, Mia pulled a hoodie over her head, the fabric warm and comforting against her skin. She didn't bother changing out of her pajama pants as she shuffled into the hall, her bare feet silent against the wood floor. At the top of the stairs, Lisa appeared, a steaming coffee mug in hand. The oversized ceramic cup bore the words *"On Mountain Time"* in bold script.

"Coffee refill," Lisa said, her voice light but uncomfortable, as though she felt the need to justify her presence. Mia raised an eyebrow. Lisa's recent habit of skipping straight to cocktails before noon hadn't gone unnoticed, and maybe this was her attempt to signal some kind of restraint.

"Did you know 20% of coffee mugs have traces of fecal matter on them?" Mia said flatly, her tone more matter-of-fact than teasing.

Right on cue, David emerged from the bathroom, his own mug in hand.

"Gross," Lisa said, wrinkling her nose. Mia wasn't sure if she was referring to the statistic or David's timing.

"Feeling better, David?" Mia asked, trying hard not to picture the microscopic particles of poop now swirling in his coffee.

"Much better," he replied, though his faint wince betrayed the words. "The migraine's gone, but I'm still dealing with the aftereffects. I'll likely sleep most of the day, but better than having a headache, though. I'll take it." He gave her a weak smile before turning back toward his room.

"David? Lisa?" Mia called after them, her voice faltering slightly.

Both paused, their attention shifting back to her.

"Did either of you hear or see anything strange last night?" she asked.

They exchanged confused glances. Lisa answered first, shaking her head. "Sorry, honey. Your dad was out cold on his meds, and I had my earplugs in."

Mia nodded, already expecting that answer. Lisa had often complained about her dad's thunderous snoring whenever he was heavily medicated for migraines. At home they rarely slept in the same room. That she hadn't mentioned his disruptive habit meant one of two things: either she was feeling unusually kind, or they'd already argued about it earlier and she didn't feel the need to rehash it.

"Why?" Lisa asked—a rare showing of concern. "Is everything okay between you kids and the staff boys?"

Jon's voice floated up from below, and Mia's pulse quickened. *He'll know something,* she thought, eager to question him. With a quick, "Fine, Lisa," response to her mother, she spun on her heel and hurried down the stairs.

At the base of the staircase, she turned toward the great room, only to stop short. Jon stood near the fireplace, his posture stiff, his gaze sharp as it passed between her and his mother. His lips pressed into a thin, silent line, and his expression warned her that now wasn't the time.

Mia hesitated, her earlier urgency colliding with a fresh wave of tension that hung heavy in the air. Whatever was going on here, it was clear Jon wasn't ready to talk—not with his mom nearby. Swallowing her frustration, Mia crossed her arms and leaned against the railing, silently vowing that she *would* get answers. Just maybe not right now.

After an uncomfortable thirty minutes of all six children picking at their breakfast while Valentina loomed over them, sensing there was something off, she finally excused herself to start a load of laundry.

Through gritted teeth, Mia scowled at Jon, "What the hell happened last night?"

Innocently, Rachel interrupted with a whisper, "Look, I don't know what shenanigans you two got into last night, but by your tone and timing, I would assume you don't want the adults to hear." She glanced up toward the balcony above. "Voices carry in this room. So I suggest you take your conversation elsewhere."

"I'll clear the table," Manny directed. "Everyone meet in the game room."

Rachel laughed in surprise, "Oh, you're in on this too?"

But, the teasing look on her face dropped after catching a serious glare from all three Miller boys and Mia.

"You need to come, too," Manny said to Rachel. "And Tenner. We all need to talk."

CHAPTER FORTY-FOUR

Rachel Johnson

NOVEMBER, 2024

Rachel sat stiffly in one of the seats around the weathered poker table, her nerves as frayed as the edge of the green felt beneath her fingers. Matthew's presence next to her should have been a comfort, but the atmosphere in the room smothered any joy she might have felt. Outside, the landscape was frozen in a merciless tableau. Unlike the soft, swirling snowfall from the previous day, the morning's ice had locked everything into eerie stillness. Branches glistened like brittle glass, and the gray sky gave the woods a suffocating, lifeless quality. Staring out the frosty window felt like peering into a noir painting—beautiful but disturbingly unnatural.

Mia leaned forward, her lips parting as if to speak, but Jon's hand shot up, silencing her before she could utter a word.

"We need to wait for Manny," Jon said, his voice low and firm. "This involves everyone."

Rachel watched as Jon glanced over at Matthew, who gave a tight, somber nod of agreement. Meanwhile, Tenner busied himself rifling through the board games stacked haphazardly on the shelves against the wall. His movements were casual, but Rachel could see the tension in his stiff shoulders. Keeping him inside for as long as they had only increased the pressure inside him. That combined with his eagerness to know what Mia and the boys were so worried about, made him a ticking time bomb. Across the table, Mia crossed her arms and slouched back in her chair, her expression a mix of frustration and defiance. Rachel tried to quell her anxiety by chewing on her nails—a habit she despised but couldn't seem to shake. Not even the occasional glance from Matthew could stop her need to self-sooth through pain.

When Manny finally entered, the air in the room shifted, though the weight of unease didn't fully lift. Instead of taking a seat, Manny leaned against the doorway, his posture tense and alert, guarding the group of teens against an unspoken threat.

"I know what I saw last night," Mia said abruptly, her voice barely above a whisper but sharp enough to cut through the thick silence.

Rachel's head jerked up, startled. "Stop being so vague! Tell us what you saw."

Mia opened her mouth to begin her explanation when John interrupted, "Mia *thought* she saw something outside last night."

Mia rolled her eyes in irritation and turned to Rachel, but Jon held up his hand again, this time asking for patience. "Let me explain," he said, his tone cautious. He took a deep breath to steady himself and looked around the room. "We are the *only* people up here on the mountain. This lodge is the *only* building around for miles. No one in their right mind would walk all the way up here, in this weather, and legally, it's private land so…"

Jon paused looking for understanding, but the sisters only stared—waiting for more.

"No doubt about it, it's creepy up here. The lodge has been *renovated,*" Jon continued using finger quotes, looking around at the shabby refurbishment, "but the bones are old. Strange noises in the night are normal. Not to mention there are wild, nocturnal animals all over the mountain."

"But," Matthew interrupted. "That being said, we can admit there's an infamous history to this place. There have been disappearances around the mountain over the past couple of years. Random people—tourists, hikers, even locals. No connections between them, no patterns. It's like they just vanish."

Rachel's stomach twisted, the memory of the missing-person posters she'd seen on the drive up flashing in her mind. "The posters," she murmured, her voice barely audible.

Matthew nodded grimly. "Yeah. And it's not only the disappearances. We've heard things—cries, footsteps, doors opening and closing in the middle of the night." Matthew quickly glanced at Jon, realizing his statement contradicted his brother's claim that the sounds were strictly a result of the aging structure. He continued, despite the stern look from Jon. "That's why none of us like staying overnight. But Mom's the boss, and she insists. It has to be one of us three, because we can't let her stay here alone at night. Whatever's going on, it actually feels safer inside than out."

His words hung in the air, heavy and suffocating. Rachel felt like the walls were closing in.

"Wait a minute," Tenner interrupted from the bookshelves. "You're telling me that you hear crazy shit, pardon my French, from here in the lodge, and you think it's *safer* for us to be *inside?*"

Mia leaned forward, her voice cutting through the silence like a blade. "There are between 25 and 50 active serial killers in the U.S. at any given time. Statistically."

Rachel dropped her head into her hands, her chest tightening as fear bubbled to the surface. She fought back the urge to cry, rubbing her eyes furiously. A hand touched her back gently, and for a moment, the soothing motion calmed her. But when she raised her head, finding Matthew staring at her concerned, his hands laced together on the table in front of him. She spun around to find Manny standing behind her.

Contrary to his touch, the look in his eyes was anything but comforting. It was sharp, almost calculating. Rachel recoiled instinctively, flinging his hand away. Her movement was abrupt enough to catch Matthew's attention. Without a word, he reached across the table and took her hand in his, his fingers intertwining with hers. The warmth of his touch steadied her, but the tension lingered like a shadow in the room.

Jon, oblivious to the undercurrent between them, pressed on. "Look, I don't know what you think you saw, Mia," he said, fixing her with a skeptical look. "But if anyone tried to leave or enter through the backdoor, we'd know. The garage door is loud as hell, and it doesn't have an automatic opener. There's no way someone snuck in or out without us hearing it. If someone really was out there, we are truly safer inside."

"I found a hidden compartment," Mia blurted out. The statement was so like the random statistics she was known to spout out that it took Rachel a moment to absorb what she had said.

"What? Where?" Tenner asked, his curiosity piqued, before Rachel could wrap her head around the statement.

"Under the bed Rachel slept in last night," Mia continued, her eyes locked on Jon's.

Rachel's heart stopped. She had slept over a hidden compartment? Her mind raced with horrifying possibilities—bones, weapons, some gruesome token of a killer's past crimes. Her breathing quickened, teetering on the edge of panic.

"Nothing was inside," Mia added, her tone flat. "But the fact it's there means there could be more. This place has secrets. I can't explain how I know. But, I know."

Tenner rolled his eyes and looked over to Rachel looking for backup. Rachel was used to Mia talking about her supposed sixth sense, her supernatural intuitiveness, and her sensitivity to the spirit world. Rachel couldn't bring herself to dismiss Mia's words this time. Something about her sister's demeanor was different—more serious, more frightened. It wasn't her usual melodramatic flair for the paranormal.

She was scared.

Mia stood, her posture rigid and commanding. "We need to search the rooms. Quietly, so the adults don't suspect anything. Tenner, you start with your room. Rachel and I will check mine. Where there is one secret, there are more!"

Jon hesitated, clearly torn between skepticism and the unsettling weight of Mia's conviction. Finally, he exhaled. "Fine. Matthew, go with Tenner. I'll check the kitchen and Manny can stay down here and keep an eye out. We don't have much time. If Mom catches us..."

"She just went to the laundry room," Manny said from the doorway, his voice low and unreadable. "You've got about fifteen minutes before she's back upstairs."

"Why can't we tell our parents?" Rachel blurted out.

Matthew sighed and looked at Rachel with compassionate understanding. "They might blame us for snooping, thinking we're getting involved in something that's none of our business. Or worse, they could accuse us of planting crazy ideas in your head and keep us apart. If we want to do this together, we have to keep our parents out of it."

"Then let's move," Mia said, her voice sharp and decisive. "We'll start with Rachel's room while Valentina is not in there."

Rachel stood reluctantly, her legs trembling as she followed Mia out of the room. Whatever secrets this lodge held, she wasn't sure she wanted to uncover them. But as she passed Matthew, his hand brushed hers again—a fleeting touch that sent a ripple of calm through her frayed nerves.

It was the last steadying thought she clung to as she followed the others out the door looking for answers she didn't want.

CHAPTER FORTY-FIVE

Caleb O' Hannegan

APRIL, 2007

The alleyway was a suffocating tomb of decay, where the air hung heavy with despair and the faint, acrid stench of garbage and piss. Towering brick walls, streaked with grime and soot, seemed to lean inward, swallowing what little light managed to filter through the narrow opening above. Shadows clung to every corner, stretching long and menacing as the distant hum of the city played like a cruel symphony of unattainable lives.

In a corner where the bricks crumbled and moss clung stubbornly to damp mortar, a tattered blue tarp sagged between rusted poles. Beneath it, a young boy by the name of Caleb O'Hannegan sat cross-legged on a threadbare blanket, his hollow eyes reflecting both the dim glow of a distant streetlamp and the deeper, more painful shadows of his young life. His oversized sweater hung limply on his frail frame, the sleeves stained and frayed. He cradled a battered toy car in his hands—a prized possession despite its missing wheel.

Caleb didn't cry—he didn't know how anymore. Tears seemed a luxury for someone with the strength to hope. At five years old, the world beyond this alley was a distant dream, one he glimpsed in the soft, warm glow of homes seen through cracked windows or the bustling figures who passed him by without a second glance. But here, in the cold embrace of the alley, life was stark and unyielding. His mother, the only constant in his short existence, was slumped over nearby.

Once vibrant and determined, his mother now appeared more shadow than human. Her coat, a patchwork of neglect, barely clung to her hunched shoulders. Her face was pale, etched with lines too deep for her years, and her dull hair clung to her forehead in limp strands. A needle dangled from the crook of her arm, the hollow echo of her addiction ringing louder than any words she had ever spoken to him.

The frail boy leaned against her still body, seeking the warmth that had once been there, but the coolness of her skin made him flinch. Above them, a steady drip from a broken pipe punctuated the suffocating silence, a cruel metronome marking the passage of time in this purgatory. Somewhere nearby, a rat darted into the shadows, its claws scratching on the pavement.

Then, the sound of approaching footsteps echoed sharply against the cobblestones. Caleb froze, his small body tensing. He didn't dare move, his mother's warning about strangers echoing faintly in his mind. A man appeared at the mouth of the alley, his silhouette tall and imposing against the faint glow of the streetlights. The tap of polished dress shoes on the wet ground sent chills down the boy's spine.

The man paused, then slowly crouched to the boy's level, his face briefly illuminated by the passing beam of a car's headlights, but otherwise shadowed. A warm smile spread across his lips, but didn't quite reach his eyes.

"Are you hungry?" the man asked softly, his voice smooth and steady.

Caleb didn't answer, his wide eyes jumping back and forth between the man and his mother. Without waiting, the stranger placed a takeout container in the boy's lap and gestured for him to open it. Hesitant but overcome by the aroma of food, he lifted the lid to reveal a warm sandwich and fries. Hunger won out over fear as he began to eat, each bite filling his empty stomach and dulling his awareness of anything else.

As Caleb ate, the man turned his attention to the boy's mother. He knelt by her side, his expression unreadable as he pressed two fingers to her neck. He let out a small sigh, shaking his head as he glanced at the needle still lodged in her arm.

When the boy finally finished his meal, his shoulders slumped in guilt. "I didn't save any for my mom," he whispered, his voice thick with regret.

The man reached out, placing a reassuring hand on the boy's shoulder. "Don't worry," he said, his tone soothing. "She would've wanted you to have it all."

Caleb's eyelids grew heavy as he leaned back onto his blanket, his small frame sinking into the cold ground. The man removed his long, puffy coat and draped it over the boy, tucking it around his body, snugly. The boy murmured a quiet thank you, his voice barely audible as exhaustion overtook him. Within moments, his breathing slowed, and his chest rose and fell in steady, peaceful rhythms.

The man stood, a faint, almost reverent smile playing on his lips. He glanced at the lifeless woman slumped against the wall, then back at the boy. "Such a sweet child," he murmured, his voice low and chilling in the quiet night. "You won't have to live without her."

He moved swiftly, stepping over the boy and bending down until his hands were wrapped tightly around the small neck. Caleb's eyes shot open in confusion and terror, but the man's grip was unrelenting. Tiny, desperate kicks rippled through the jacket as the boy struggled, but the man only closed his eyes, his face a mask of eerie calm,

The man always knew he had it in him—the ability to take the life of another human. But, he had no idea how it would make him feel. The God-like power excited him as the boy stared back at him—the young boy's life literally in his hands. The thought crossed his mind to let go—save the boy. The thought of playing with his prey excited him—the way a cat plays with a wounded bird. As euphoria surged through him, he let out a small laugh and tightened his grip. This feeling could prove addictive.

When the struggle ceased, and the alley returned to its dreadful silence, the man stood once more, adjusting his cuffs with meticulous care. He gazed down at the boy, now forever still, and whispered, "Together again." Then, without a backward glance, he disappeared into the shadows, leaving the alley even more lifeless than before.

CHAPTER FORTY-SIX

Mia Johnson

NOVEMBER, 2024

Mia sank back on her heels, stretching her arms toward the ceiling in a vain attempt to loosen the tension gripping her muscles. She'd spent a solid ten minutes crawling across the floor of Rachel's room, pressing on every single floorboard, and the ache in her body was relentless. Across the room, Rachel had long ago abandoned the task. She now sat at the desk, doodling aimlessly with her colorful highlighters, her focus drifting in and out.

Mia rolled her neck, exhaling a deep sigh as her arms fell back to her sides. In the daylight, their search felt absurd. Why was she so desperate to find answers? A string of missing persons in some remote mountain town didn't have to mean anything sinister nor did it necessarily relate to the lodge. People had their reasons for leaving, didn't they? If she lived in an old mountain town, she may run away as well. And the strange noises at night? Nothing but the quirks of an old house. The whole search seemed more like a stir-crazy way to keep themselves busy. Their family would be gone soon anyway.

But then her gaze drifted to her hands, pressed flat against the worn hardwood. A shiver ran up her arm, raising goosebumps as her thoughts lingered on her nightmare combined with what she'd seen the night before. That shadowy figure outside. She might have dismissed it, chalked it up to her imagination, if it weren't for the way he had turned. And looked directly at her. From far below, through the darkness, as if feeling the pressure of her stare from stories above.

She couldn't ignore that. Something deep in her gut told her the missing people, the mysterious stranger, and Matthew, Jon, and Manny's missing sister were all connected somehow.

Gripping the edge of the pristinely made bed for support, Mia hoisted herself up, muscles protesting the movement. She'd lie down for a moment before tackling the next room. But as her fingers brushed against something hard and smooth in the space between the mattress and boxspring, she felt a sharp poke.

"Ow!" She jerked her hand back, instinctively placing the stinging finger in her mouth. The bitter tang of iron hit her tongue, making her grimace. Pulling her hand away, she studied the thin, red line running across her fingertip. It wasn't deep, but it burned.

"Butterflies like drinking blood," Mia muttered.

Then, realization struck.

Ignoring the pain, she reached back under the mattress. Her fingers found the object again—something solid, rectangular, and unfamiliar. With a quick tug, she freed it.

A book. No. A journal.

Its leather cover was smooth and well-worn, its spine creased from use. A jumble of colorful sticky notes jutted from the pages, along with a sharp, oddly stretched paperclip was wedged among them. For a moment, Mia stared at it, her breath caught in her throat.

"What is it?" Rachel's voice broke through the silence.

"I... found something," Mia murmured, barely audible.

Rachel must have sensed the weight of the discovery, because she slid her chair back without a word and joined Mia on the floor. The sisters sat side by side, the journal resting on Mia's knees like a forbidden artifact.

Rachel had been journaling since she was young and though she forbade Mia from reading them, she had seen the progression of journal styles. What started as colorful and cartoonish designs had morphed into covers adorned with photos of stunning landscapes and inspirational quotes. But, even through Rachel's maturing journal tastes, she had not yet reached the level of high-end leather bound. The book she held was not one owned by a teenager.

"This isn't yours, is it?" Mia asked, her voice uncertain.

Rachel shook her head, her eyes locked on the book. "Not mine. And definitely not the kind of thing I'd expect someone to leave behind."

Mia nodded, tracing her fingers along the soft leather. "If it were simply forgotten, it would've been in the nightstand. Or on the desk. Maybe even under the bed. But under the mattress? Someone hid this."

Rachel's brow furrowed, her voice dropping to a whisper. "Why would they need to hide it?"

"I don't know," Mia said, her voice hardening. "But I don't think it was an accident."

They exchanged a tense look, the unspoken question hanging between them.

Rachel took the journal out of Mia's hands and moved to open it.

Mia reached forward, her hand hovering over the cover. "Let's keep looking. If we found this there is probably more."

"What? No," Rachel nearly shouted. "This is a really big deal. We need to tell everyone." Rachel paused as if searching for a reaction, but Mia gave none, intent on searching while they still had some daylight coming in through the windows. The lodge had electricity but the bulbs were weak and what the evening lighting did for ambiance had the opposite effect on clarity.

Rachel stepped closer to Mia. "Didn't Matthew say that their dad bought Ana a journal to help her cope with her feelings about him getting sick?"

Then, with a deep breath, Mia flipped the journal open. The page greeted them with handwriting so deliberate and precise.

A pink sticky note sat dead center of the first page, covering what looked like part of the journal owner's contact information. Two words were written in a shaky hand, a sharp contrast to the writing that lay beneath.

Murder Manor.

CHAPTER FORTY-SEVEN

Rachel Johnson

NOVEMBER, 2024

Frantic coughing echoed up the stairs and carried into the room. Rachel and Mia exchanged a glance before quickly standing in panic as the sound of someone walking up the stairs got louder. The sisters hid behind the door, their eyes frantically searching for an escape.

"Manny, mi hijo. Are you choking or something?" Manny's coughing had stopped Valentina's ascent, but he continued his hacking.

"Let me get you some tea with honey," Valentina said sweetly.

Rachel let her head drop back against the wall at the sound of Valentina retreating to the kitchen. After a quick peek into the hallway, Mia scampered out, snatching the journal from Rachel and tucking it in the front pocket of her hoodie.

Rachel quietly pulled the door closed behind her, hoping they had left no evidence in their wake. When she turned, she walked straight into Matthew.

"Nothing in...," Matthew started.

"Oh my gosh!" Rachel exhaled.

She dropped her eyes, laughing through the embarrassment.

"Mia's waiting downstairs," Rachel started again, looking over his shoulder. "Where's Tenner?"

"Um," Matthew looked over his shoulder back to Tenner's room, rubbing his hand over the back of his neck. "Oh, he's going to meet us in the game room."

The slight blush was visible even against his gorgeous flawless skin. The heat between them gave Rachel unexpected confidence.

"Let's go," Rachel said directly and grabbed Matthew's hand, pulling him down the stairs behind her.

His body was tense and after watching him take another glance over his shoulder, this time towards the only unoccupied room at the end of the hall–Mr. Murdoch's room. She began to wonder if his blush was from her or something else entirely. He seemed nervous, and not in a "cute little crush" way.

His cough miraculously gone, Manny was still standing at the door, like a watch dog, his eyes roaming in a non-stop search for threats. Or parents.

Jon and Mia sat at the table where Rachel and Matthew took a seat.

"Where's Tenner," Mia asked Rachel.

"He'll be here," Rachel answered with a backward glance at Matthew. He'd taken a seat and didn't raise his eyes back to her. He no longer looked nervous, he looked suspicious.

Jon looked impatiently around the table. "Did anyone find anything?"

Mia looked towards the open doorway as if willing Tenner to enter.

"He probably went to get a snack," Rachel chimed in sensing Mia's unease.

"Did anyone find anything?" Jon asked again louder.

Mia looked back to the table, opting to get started without Tenner. "Rachel and I found a journal."

"A journal?" Manny asked from the door, taking a step into the room, more animated than Rachel had ever seen him.

"Is it pink?" Matthew asked, suddenly more alert sitting straighter in his chair.

Mia pulled the leather book out from her front hoodie pocket and placed it on the table in front of her. Manny turned back to the door, shielding his face as Matthew's entire body relaxed back into his chair, a look of disappointment passing over his face.

"It was hidden between the mattress and the boxspring in Rachel's room. Seems like a strange place to store your journal. And on top of that, if you have a journal important enough for you to hide it, how could you possibly forget it?"

Rachel didn't have a response to that. It was certainly suspicious but if Mia was so sure someone else was around and she was trying to get to the bottom of the strange sounds, then what did that have to do with a hidden journal?

Mia leaned forward, flipped open the first page, then spun the book around so everyone at the table could see the sticky note.

"Murder Manor." Matthew read in a whisper, picking up and inspecting the book. "This has to be from someone who has visited since the lodge reopened. No way this is over 50 years old."

"There have only been a handful of guests since we opened," Jon began. He leaned back and held up his hand counting off his fingers. "There was that couple that came. They stayed in the room your parents are in."

"The bachelorette party," Matthew chimed in. "But, I can't remember anyone even asking about the house or its history. All they wanted to do was drink. I seriously doubt any of them were undercover investigators."

"What about the journalist?" Manny asked from the doorway.

Matthew turned in his seat to look at his brother. "She cancelled though, right?"

"No, she didn't cancel. She just didn't show up," Jon clarified.

"Oh, that's right, Matthew said. I was supposed to work overnight but when she didn't show up, Murdoch sent me home." Matthew spoke with confidence but he appeared uneasy.

"The cops came by looking for her," Manny said, his eyes on the back of Matthew's head. "They said her family and co-workers were concerned and this was the last place she had been. They all thought she checked in but never checked out."

"What?" Jon exclaimed. "You never told us that."

"Yeah. I guess I forgot," Manny replied. " I was here when they came by. It was a couple patrol guys. I called Murdoch to come up from town and he talked to them. Told me it was all a big misunderstanding."

Rachel's eyes moved back and forth between the brothers trying to absorb all the facts. The facts that were forming a clear picture in her head, but seemed to be eluding the others at the table. Rachel reached across the table and grabbed the journal. She flipped through the pages that were covered in detailed notes and newspaper clippings. The academic side of her wanted to look through each page in methodical detail, but she fought the urge and flipped to the inside cover where the owner's contact information was located.

"Do you remember her name?" Rachel asked without looking up.

Matthew looked over her shoulder and down at the name. "Yup. That's her."

CHAPTER FORTY-EIGHT

Mia Johnson

NOVEMBER, 2024

The journal belonged to a journalist by the name of Ella Whitmore. She was booked to stay one night at Murdoch Manor, but according to Matthew and Manny, she never showed up. Finding the stashed journal upstairs, however, told a different story. Matthew mentioned that he was sent home early since their scheduled lodger was a no-show. But, he also added that Murdoch went back down to the valley at the same time.

"Did you follow him to the town? Do you know he actually left?" Mia asked.

"Well, not exactly. I was here alone that day because there were no guests at the time so my job was to prepare for Ms. Whitmore and spend the night. I thought it was odd at the time that my mom wasn't here to prepare dinner. That's pretty standard for all guests unless they plan in advance to be a late arrival. But, if she had notified him that she would be arriving late, why would he send me home early?" Matthew stumbled on his words, trying to remember clearly. "But, I'm sure he left. As I pulled out of the driveway, I saw him locking up in my rearview mirror. He was leaving right behind me." Matthew looked around the table as if someone would give him the answer he wanted.

"Maybe she showed up late. No one was here. She dropped her journal as she left and the next guest picked it up, a kid maybe, and hid it like a treasure. Regardless of whether this woman showed up or not, a journal that was left behind has nothing to do with the strange sounds we've been hearing or the person Mia saw roaming around outside last night," Rachel piped up injecting logic before the theories got out of hand.

Manny walked over to the table and grabbed the journal, opening it up to the marked page. "You don't find it the slightest bit coincidental that the journal that was *dropped*," he said adding quote fingers, "just happened to be about Murder Manor?"

"Hi kids," Valentina popped into the room, her energy lower than it had been, and her smile looking more forced than ever.

Manny turned and held the journal behind his back.

"Hi, mom," Jon said as he stood up from the table. "Do you need us?"

"Oh no," Valentina brushed off the offer. "I have tea with honey for Manny's cough and wanted to call you all to lunch." She paused momentarily looking embarrassed. "Okay, maybe it's closer to dinner. Sorry that it's so late. I got so busy running laundry that I lost all track of time."

While Jon moved toward his mom, Manny slowly backed away, deeper into the room.

Jon hugged her and relieved her of the tea cup and saucer, "We can handle ourselves, mom. Why don't you take a break."

Valentina eyed her boys suspiciously, then looked at Mia and her siblings. Every kid in that room wore the guilty look of a kid caught with their hand in the cookie jar. Rachel's eyes were wide open with fright, more afraid of getting caught snooping by Valentina than whatever they thought they may find in Ella's journal.

Valentina clapped her hands three times, the loud noise echoing through the room and breaking the group from their trance.

"Well, let's go," Valentina added, with more zest than when she entered. "What are you waiting for? Chop, chop."

Valentina stood at the door as Matthew stood and walked out after Jon and Rachel. As Mia calmly stepped around the table to follow the group out of the game room, she saw Manny slide the journal between two board games on the bookshelf.

CHAPTER FORTY-NINE

Rachel Johnson

NOVEMBER, 2024

The table was empty. Not a platter, glass, or bowl in sight. Without Valentina's usual decorations, the long banquet table looked more like a sacrificial altar than a place to dine. The thought was morbid but Rachel knew she wasn't alone in her thinking when Mia said, "Many ancient cultures sacrifice virgins to ensure good fortune."

"Didn't have a chance to bring everything out," Valentina said as she followed the group into the great room. "The food is on the counter in the kitchen. Grab a plate and help yourself."

Matthew turned and waited for Rachel. His eyes held an apology, as if he were somehow responsible for the storm—or the entire mess they were caught in. As she approached, he extended his hand, and without hesitation, she took it, letting him guide her into the kitchen. The weight of his hand in hers felt suddenly familiar—less awkward than before. Her fascination with him, the way her body responded to his presence, still burned strong. But now, instead of fighting it, she could finally let herself feel it.

Leftover burgers and chicken breasts sat on a plate next to a bag of buns and storage containers with day-old salad. It was far from the fancy spread Valentina had been spoiling them with, but it wasn't as if she could head out for groceries. No one looked hungry, simply plating their food to appease Valentina. Rachel was itching to get back at the journal, to scour the pages, read the articles, and solve the mystery of Ella Whitmore. She may have argued that the journal had little to do with the noises and mysterious figure outside but that didn't mean she wouldn't bury herself in the journal, avoiding food, water, and sleep, until she reached the end.

"Rachel," Matthew was staring at her, concern wrinkling his forehead. "You okay?"

Rachel blushed and looked down at her empty plate and then behind her to everyone else who was waiting for her so they could get their food.

"Burger or chicken?" Rachel laughed awkwardly, "almost as hard as picking a college?"

Mia rolled her eyes, and ducked behind Jon hiding from the second-hand embarrassment.

Rachel grabbed a cheeseburger, bun, and a scoop of wilted lettuce, then turned toward the kitchen door. Matthew jumped in front of her, gracefully balancing his plate and holding the door open for her.

Matthew, Jon, and Manny sat on one side of the table while Rachel and Mia sat on the other. The five sat in silence and ate as Valentina hovered over them from outside the kitchen door.

When Valentina was finally satisfied that the children in the lodge were being fed, albeit in silence, she kissed each of her boys on the head, spoke something in hushed Spanish and disappeared through the swinging door.

"Is she okay?" Rachel asked, directing her question towards the boys across the table.

"I think she's just tired. The last few days have been longer than normal," Jon answered without looking up from his plate.

"She'll be okay in the morning. She'll take a sleeping pill, get a good night's sleep and wake up fresh and ready to go," Matthew said.

"She gets like this when she spends too much time up here. It's like she mourns the loss of Ana more the higher up the mountain she gets," Manny added.

Mia coughed, the water catching in her throat. The sound was loud in the quiet dining room, sharp enough to draw every eye at the table. For a beat, no one spoke. The clink of silverware stopped midair. They all waited, as if expecting her to break the silence with one of her typically ill-timed remarks—something too blunt, too curious, too inappropriate for dinner.

But instead, she swallowed hard, steadied herself, and asked, "What was she like? Ana? You know... before..."

The word *before* hung there like smoke.

Rachel felt the air shift. She inhaled sharply, spine locking straight, ready for someone—anyone—to tell Mia to mind her own business. Or worse, to stand up, leave the table, and end the evening in the kind of silence that says too much.

But that didn't happen.

The brothers—Matthew, Manny, and Jon—exchanged quiet glances. To Rachel's surprise, something soft cracked through their solemn expressions. Small, wistful smiles formed.

Matthew leaned back in his chair, the corners of his mouth lifting first. "We're all close in age," he said. "But Ana, being the oldest, always thought she had to be the responsible one. She wanted to take care of us."

He gave a short laugh, and the sound loosened the tension just enough for the others to breathe.

"Her idea of taking care of us," he continued, "usually meant bossing us around. But she loved us fiercely. There was never a doubt about that."

Manny's voice came next, low and warm with memory. "In fourth grade, some punk-ass kid told everyone he was gonna beat me up after school. Word got around to Ana. I don't even know how—she had this sixth sense when it came to us. She showed up at the gate that day, backpack slung over one shoulder, ready to throw down."

Jon laughed, sudden and loud. "God, the look on her face! Like she'd been waiting her whole life for someone to mess with her family." His grin spread, and for a moment, the table felt alive again. "She was fueled with pride and pure adrenaline. I swear, she could've tackled an elephant if she needed to."

The laughter faded slowly, replaced by an ache that settled over them with long, resigned sighs.

Matthew's smile faltered. "She was caring," he said quietly. "Loyal. And no matter how she felt before she left... she would've loved this place."

Jon nodded, his eyes darkening. "Ana and Mom... they were so much alike. That's probably why they fought sometimes. But if they'd ever run this place together—like Mom planned—it would've been everything they both wanted."

His voice broke on the last word. He looked down at his lap, shoulders sinking.

Silence filled the space again. This time it wasn't peaceful—it was heavy, almost unbearable. The kind of silence that makes you want to move just to prove you're still there.

Finally, Matthew pushed back his chair and stood, gathering the plates. The scrape of porcelain against wood was too loud in the quiet room.

"Hold up," Mia said, her voice cutting through the hush. "Where are you going? We need to talk about the journal."

"Who has it?" Rachel demanded.

Matthew, Jon, and Rachel looked around the table, from one person to another, while Mia's eyes bore into Manny's forehead while he pushed soggy salad around on his plate.

Mia stood suddenly and spun around, searching the room.

"Where's Tenner?"

CHAPTER FIFTY

Mia Johnson

NOVEMBER, 2024

"Maybe he fell asleep," Rachel chimed in.

It seemed unlikely. There wasn't a human on earth that could go with less sleep than Tenner. Never in his life had Mia ever seen him take a nap, or go to bed early. Even on the rare occasion when he had gone to his room at night and not returned to his parents for a snack or with a question, he stayed up watching videos on his phone until early in the morning.

"Rachel," Mia pressed. "When did he tell you he would meet us in the game room?"

Rachel's eyes opened wider before she turned a worried expression to Matthew who was uncharacteristically bobbling the plates as he tried to make a quick exit to the kitchen.

"Matthew?" Rachel asked, her voice timid, full of concern.

Matthew stopped before the kitchen door, took a deep breath and turned, placing the dirty plates back on the table.

"Look, Tenner and I went upstairs together to search his room, but when we got there, he gave me this whole *I don't need a babysitter* speech and said he would find answers on his own."

He looked around at the others, Mia and Rachel suddenly ramrod straight.

"Who am I to argue? I'm not his dad," Matthew reached up and nervously rubbed the back of his neck, his eyes dropping to the dirty dishes that were becoming more enticing by the second. Anything to escape the tension and stares.

Mia left her plate behind and ran up the stairs two at a time, while Rachel sprinted for the front door.

As Mia reached the top of the stairs, she heard Rachel yell from the foyer, "No footprints out here."

The doors along the hallway were closed, and no light shone from underneath. The setting sun was doing little to help her nerves. Never one to be afraid of the dark, she was oddly shaken. Her stomach roiled and she knew at once it had nothing to do with the burger. Something was wrong. She could feel it. The entire second floor seemed to be closing in on her. The dark carpet and thick wallpaper only added to the heavy atmosphere.

Without a knock or courtesy "excuse me", Mia threw open the bathroom door. Finding it empty, she ran her hand over the base of the sink. There were water droplets but then again Valentina had just gone to bed. She moved to the shower and tossed the curtain aside, finding the floor of the shower bone dry.

How long had it been since she'd seen him? He left with Matthew to search his room. How long had it been? Hours? She couldn't think straight. Certainly if he had come up to take a shower in the last hour there would be residual water drops or even a foggy mirror, but two hours?

Mia stormed out of the bathroom and slammed open Tenner's door. If he somehow found WiFi and was hiding in his room, she would be pissed. But, when she looked around, all she found was an empty room.

CHAPTER FIFTY-ONE

Rachel Johnson

NOVEMBER, 2024

No footprints were left behind in the snow and with the flurries no longer falling, it was doubtful that anyone had stepped outdoors that afternoon. Leaving no stone unturned, Rachel verified that Tenner's shoes were still by the door. And dry.

She ran into the game room only to find Manny standing with his back to the bookshelf.

"What are you doing?" Rachel practically yelled. "Why aren't you looking for Tenner?"

"Oh, um. I just wanted to check something in the journal." He paused, his expression turning oddly compassionate. "Did you want help? I assumed he was upstairs or something."

"I'm sure he's fine," Matthew said as he entered the room earning him a scolding look from Jon who walked in behind him. "He's obviously in the house."

Rachel plopped down in a chair and folded her arms on the table, her head falling to rest on top. "You don't understand." Her words came out muffled as she spoke into her arms. Taking another deep breath, she looked up. "He likes to explore, try crazy tricks... the kid thinks he's invincible. Just because he's never had a bad fall or seems to always land on his feet, doesn't mean bad things can't happen."

"Bad things?" Matthew questioned with a small smirk. "What do you think could possibly happen? Yeah, we're stuck in a storm, but we're inside, we have electricity, food, and water. Even if he's exploring the basement, he'll find his way back up."

Jon and Manny shot a warning look at their brother while Rachel asked, "There's a basement?"

Rachel looked back and forth between the boys, their expressions revealing more than their words as Mia rounded the reception desk towards them.

"Yeah," Jon confirmed. "Where do you think the back door is?"

"Mia," Rachel stated. "There's a basement."

Mia stared at her as if what she said was ridiculous. "Yeah. Obviously. Have you seen the hill this place is built into? The ground outside is level with the front porch but outside my bedroom window has to be a 30 to 40 foot drop."

Rachel wanted to argue or even defend herself, burning from embarrassment. Of course there's a basement. She should've put that together on her own. She was the smart one after all.

Rachel ran a hand over her face, trying to compose herself. "We need to tell mom and dad. Then we need to search the basement."

CHAPTER FIFTY-TWO

Mia Johnson

NOVEMBER, 2024

"Don't bother," Mia rolled her eyes.

Mia had peeked into her parents' room while she was upstairs, hoping—desperately—that for some strange reason, Tenner might be in there. He wasn't. The air was stale, thick with the sour mix of body odor, mildew, and wine. Clothes were strewn across the floor like ant hills, chaotic and teetering. Mia stepped carefully, not out of concern for the mess, but for her own safety. She knew better than to bother her dad—he was out cold, an eye mask and headphones sealing him off from the world. He wouldn't be waking until morning.

What surprised her was her mom—mouth wide open, snoring, with a slick thread of drool spreading a dark stain across her pillow. Back home, her mom only drank socially. But something had unraveled this week, pushing her to the bottom of her wine glass like she was searching for a way out.

"Dad's medicine knocked him out," Mia said. "I tried waking Mom. I thought maybe she was just resting—she didn't even eat dinner. But when I shook her, she jolted awake for like two seconds, mumbled something about smash burgers and Valentina's sleeping pills, then passed out again."

Jon rolled his eyes, glancing at his brothers. Both of them looked away.

"Since Ana…" he trailed off.

They all knew what he meant. How any mother could get a moment's rest knowing her daughter might still be out there was beyond Mia. But *she* knew better. Ana wasn't out there. She was *here*—somewhere inside this rotting, cursed lodge. Watching. Waiting. And for all intents and purposes, she was alone, unseen by the people who were supposed to love her most.

A chill ran up Mia's spine at the thought of Tenner.

"I'm going to search the basement," she said, even though she had no clue how to get there.

Jon stood, placing a steadying hand on her shoulder. "No. Matthew and I will go. It's not heated and gets freezing down there. We know the way and can move faster than you could."

He shot Matthew a sharp look, a silent order. Matthew rose and joined him at the door. Jon turned to Manny.

"You. Stay with them. Don't let them out of your sight."

Rachel's shoulders slumped, her face crumpling. She looked like she might cry. She was almost an adult—only a couple years from living on her own. Why did she seem so breakable?

"There's a one-in-three chance your killer is never identified if you're murdered in the U.S.," Mia said flatly.

"That's not helping, Mia," Rachel muttered, her voice small and wounded.

Mia sighed. She needed Rachel focused, not unraveling. That mind of hers could solve anything—if she could just stay calm.

"We'll find him before Mom and Dad wake up," Mia said. Then she turned to Manny, who stood by the bookcase with his hands awkwardly behind his back. "Manny, get that journal you're hiding and bring it over. We may as well find out what's in there while we wait."

CHAPTER FIFTY-THREE

Ella Whitmore

OCTOBER, 2024

Ella drove up the bumpy road, replaying her conversation with Josh, the waiter, again and again. He'd brought two drinks and joined her at the table. They talked for nearly thirty minutes—right up until his boss returned.

"What do you know about the Hilltop Escape?" Josh had asked as he sat down.

"That's literally what I'm asking *you*," Ella had replied.

Josh rubbed a hand over his face. "I mean—where'd you hear that name? Most locals are tight-lipped about the whole thing. And for those of us born after 1980, all we've got is gossip."

"Okay," Ella said slowly. "So what can you tell me?"

"Are you a reporter or something?"

"Actually, yes. Investigative journalist." Ella slid her card across the table.

Josh glanced at it, then leaned in. "Look, I don't know much—like I said, just the rumors. But from what I've heard, the guy who ran the place was torturing people."

"Yeah, I know that part," Ella said, cutting him off. "What I *want* to know is, why—when I search for the hotel—it's like it never existed. Not even an address."

"Oh, right," Josh said, leaning back in his chair. "So, I guess the place shut down when that guy went to prison. It sat empty for years—decades, really. Just rotted up there on that hill. Then out of nowhere, some guy comes along, fixes it up, and renames everything—the hotel—now Murdoch Manor. He even went so far as to change the names of the mountain and roads. Like he wanted to erase its history."

"I hear there's no internet up there," Josh had warned before he got up to busy himself when his boss returned. "A few local guys I know work there during the day."

Then he bent low, pretending to clear the table, and whispered, "No one can know I talked to you about this. People around here are really, *really* weird about it."

He stood back up, slipped his glass into the front pocket of his apron, then picked up her plate and glass. "Can I get you anything else?" he asked, voice neutral, as if nothing had passed between them.

After leaving the café, Ella had stopped by the library to get internet access. She managed to book a room at the lodge for that night—which turned out to be a good thing. When she returned to her B&B, the front door was still locked, and Meemaw had left Ella's bag packed and sitting on the front porch.

As eager as she was to get up the mountain and see the place for herself, Ella took a little extra time at the library. She searched prison records.

There were no files on an *Elias Thornfield*.

But after the total lack of information on everything else, she wasn't exactly surprised.

On the drive up the mountain, Ella made a decision: no one at the lodge could know about her investigation. She was certain they'd want to keep any dark history buried—bad for business, unless the owner was trying to attract true crime junkies.

She hoped she'd be able to slip in and out of rooms, searching the place without drawing attention. But she'd have to be discreet.

Still, if she ever wanted to make a name for herself, this was the kind of risk she had to take. The *Journalism Safety* course would have a field day tearing her plan apart—but no journalist ever made a name by playing it safe.

Chapter Fifty-Four

Mia Johnson

November, 2024

Rachel flipped frantically through the journal, speed reading while Mia tried to digest bits and pieces before the pages were flipped.

"It's all about this place," Rachel summarized after the first ten pages or so. "Her notes detail stories about stuff that happened up here in the mid twentieth century. Looks like all urban legends and campfire stories. I don't see anywhere she has proof or documentation of any of this."

Mia leaned over to Rachel. "I thought you were going to take notes."

"I am," Rachel said with a smile tapping her temple with her pointer finger.

Mia rolled her eyes. "People with high IQs are more likely to develop a mental illness."

Rachel turned to Manny, "When was her reservation?"

Manny stepped out to the lobby to confirm the date and verified there were no other reservations that day.

"That was over a month ago," Rachel exclaimed. "Is it possible no one ran across the journal? I know it was hidden, but not that well."

Manny averted his gaze, red shame washing over his face. "I mean, we change the sheets and stuff, but it's not like we flip the mattresses between guests." He signed deeply. "Plus, we haven't exactly been booked every day."

Mia looked up at Manny, knowing there was more he wasn't saying.

"So, how many people stayed in Rachel's room before her?" Mia asked.

"Well," Manny began. "There was the journalist, who I'll remind you that I never saw. There was a bachelorette party. We each stayed one night during their three night stay, but I can't be sure who stayed in that specific room." Manny cleared his throat before looking up at Rachel and adding, under his breath, "Then you."

"Wait!" Rachel spoke louder than she intended. "Are you telling us that only two people potentially stayed in that room before we came? You guys act like all this mysterious stuff happens *every* time you stay, as if you've stayed overnight so often."

Manny pushed his chair back and walked aggressively toward the window. "We spent most of our life in that town down the mountain. The four of us practically grew up hearing tales of missing people, monsters, and murder up on this mountain. Those stories in the journal? I have heard every one of them—over a hundred times—I have no idea if any of it is true, but living under the shadow of a mountain with a mysterious history... it gets to you. "

Manny walked back to the table and took a seat, propping his elbows on the table and lacing his fingers together. "No. None of us want to stay. Between the three of us we have 2 rules. Never go out at night. And stay in your room after dark. I know we're supposed to be 'on-call' for the guests but we haven't been tested yet. Those women who stayed, passed out cold every night. But, I can tell you from experience, being in this place with 6 unconscious women is very much like being here alone. And when you're all alone..."

Rachel finished his sentence, "everything is amplified."

Mia added, "Every animal noise from outside, or creaky noise from inside."

Manny nodded. "When those cops came by asking about the journalist, I didn't think anything of it. Murdoch said she never showed. So, I assumed she never showed. He's a weird dude but have you seen him? Dude couldn't hurt a fly. He's one dimensional."

"So, what are you saying then?" Mia threw back at him. "Are you saying that Murdoch really thought she didn't show up, and moseyed his skinny ass back down to the village while she broke in and stayed alone."

Rachel raised a finger to interrupt but Mia continued, "No, not just that. But, she stayed, alone, left without a trace, and wait for it... before she left, she hid her journal. Why? In case some other curious traveller wanted a maybe-true historical background of the place?"

Mia grabbed the journal from Rachel and held it up. "This is proof she was here. She did show up. She knew something about this place. And she never made it home."

"Technically we don't know if she made it home. The cops came by weeks ago. Maybe she's home by now," Manny added, doubting even his own words.

Mia slammed the journal down onto the table and pushed her seat back with such force, it overturned on the ground behind her. Leaving the chair in her wake, she turned towards the doorway. She had to find Tenner. This waiting was driving her crazy and who cares about a seventy-five year old story. Her brother was missing.

"Mia." Rachel's soft voice called out behind her.

"What?" Mia demanded, not bothering to turn around.

When no answer came, she spun toward Rachel and Manny, who were leaning over the open journal. It was flipped well past the last of the earlier stories, toward blank pages at the back. Mia hurried the few steps to join them.

The writing wasn't like the polished prose in the front of the journal. These pages were sparse, filled with haphazard scribbles, and the first note she saw sent a chill down her spine:

He's going to kill me.

CHAPTER FIFTY-FIVE

Rachel Johnson

NOVEMBER, 2024

Goosebumps covered Rachel's arms, and her eyes watered out of fright. But, there was nothing that would stop her from reading what was next.

I broke in

Closet has fake floor

Documents/ Proof

Murder Manor was real

Elias Thornfield arrested and convicted of torturing and killing in lodge

No internet record! Erased?

Daughter was given the property. Never came. Died in 2022.

"2022!" Manny exclaimed. "That's when my mom wanted to buy this place." His face dropped, excitement leaving his body as he fell back into a chair. "And when Ana went missing."

"What does this mean?" Mia asked.

Rachel read over the text again and again. None of it made sense. She was trying to solve a puzzle without all the pieces. She read each line again, this time aloud, "*I broke in*. So, she did break into the lodge. She must've heard all the stories and came up to investigate. Maybe she was disappointed to find it had reopened and just lucked out that the place wasn't fully booked."

"I don't know." Manny replied skeptically. "She actually had a reservation, so why would she have to break in? Plus, Murdoch is pretty careful about locking up when no one's here."

"What about your mom?" Mia asked Manny.

Manny's eyes dimmed from dark to darker as he met Mia's. A scowl crossed his face and he looked as if he would jump over the table and eat Mia whole.

"*Closet has fake floor*." Rachel read the next line, hoping to diffuse the tension and bring them back to the journal. "Manny, do you know of a fake floor anywhere?"

Before Manny could answer, Mia chimed in, "There was that small compartment in my room. But, that was under the bed in the middle of a room, not in a closet."

"Yeah," Rachel brushed her hand towards Mia. "But, we know nothing was in there. Manny?"

Manny, having regained his composure, sighed. "Look. If I'd found a ton of revealing documents behind a fake floor, I'd have told you by now. Plus, none of the guest rooms even have closets."

"Okay, so no documents, no fake floor, no closets, no one witnessing her even being here. So, what does the next part mean?" Mia asked, now pacing around the room.

"Well, I think it must mean that the stories are true. This guy tortured and killed people here, but for one reason or another there is no online proof. I would think even though it happened before the internet, that there would still be something, old scanned newspapers, arrest warrants, microfiche, something, right?" Rachel's mind was spinning. Only seeing part of a picture can be misleading. What were they missing?

Distant running could be heard across the house and Rachel stood to see who was coming, willing it to be Tenner. When Rachel felt someone would push through the kitchen door any second, Mia grabbed the journal and flipped to the backside of the page. Two words stared back at them—in the same, panicked writing.

He knows.

CHAPTER FIFTY-SIX

Mia Johnson

NOVEMBER, 2024

Jon and Matthew burst into the room. Alone. No Tenner.

Both of their faces were pale and strained, like they'd seen a ghost. And maybe they had.

A translucent Ana lingered behind her brothers, her eyes locked on Mia with an expression that almost looked like a plea. Had they seen her? Mia glanced at Manny, searching his face for any sign of recognition—but there was nothing. When she turned back, Ana was gone.

"Tenner?" Rachel asked, her voice barely a squeak.

Jon shook his head, and Matthew gently pulled Rachel into his side as she buried her face against his chest.

"We came up to get flashlights," Jon said, his voice tight. "It's pitch black down there."

"We're coming too," Mia called after them as they turned to go. "More eyes, better chances. I can't sit here with this journal any longer. We need to find Tenner."

CHAPTER FIFTY-SEVEN

Rachel Johnson

NOVEMBER, 2024

"Take us down," Rachel demanded, shrugging off Matthew's touch.

Now wasn't the time to cozy up to him or give in to the butterflies fluttering in her gut. She had to be strong.

The three brothers and Mia turned to her, stunned. A strange calm had settled over her. She was laser-focused now, certain that if she could look for herself, she'd find something the others had missed.

"Now!" she snapped.

Jon turned and jogged toward the kitchen, Rachel close behind, not even glancing to see if the others followed.

They pushed through the swinging door, rushed across the kitchen, and entered a narrow back hallway. An old door hung open on its hinges at the end, revealing a dark stairwell that led into the basement. A rush of cold air spilled out, flooding the hallway like a threat of what lay below.

Jon paused at the top of the stairs, looking back at her as if to ask if she was sure. But before he could say a word, she snatched the flashlight from his hand and started down the narrow steps.

At the bottom, Rachel stood in the center of the room and slowly turned, letting the flashlight sweep over every corner. The concrete floor was freezing—the chill creeping through her shoes. The scent of mildew hung beneath the faint aroma of fresh laundry.

The others followed her down. Matthew approached and pulled the cord dangling above her head, flicking on a single bulb that bathed the basement in dim yellow light.

Along one wall sat two industrial-sized washers and dryers. Beside them, a wooden clothesline stretched across the space, holding pressed, cloth placemats and napkins. Further down, an ironing board supported an old iron and a dust-covered bottle of starch.

The wall farthest from the stairs was nearly bare, except for a roll-up garage-style door.

The opposite wall was lined with refrigerators and freezers of different sizes. Rachel swallowed hard, forcing herself to move. With every step, the deep freezer at the far end seemed to drift farther away, tunnel vision making her dizzy, her breath short.

Matthew stepped beside her and gently wrapped an arm around her waist, turning her around.

"It's okay. There's nothing in them but food," he said softly.

"I have to see," Rachel replied, her voice steadier now, the spark of courage returning.

She turned back and stepped forward, then grabbed the handle of the deep freezer and yanked it open.

A rush of breath escaped her chest. Inside: frozen chicken, steak, and pizzas—nothing else. Still, she didn't stop. She checked each freezer, one by one. As Matthew had said, they were filled with food—nothing else.

But something was wrong.

She couldn't explain it— a feeling crawling up her spine. Something about the room didn't make sense.

She turned in a slow circle, scanning everything again. Then it hit her.

"Where's the rest of the basement?"

CHAPTER FIFTY-EIGHT

Mia Johnson

NOVEMBER, 2024

Mia should've figured it out sooner. She'd spent countless nights sitting by her bedroom window, staring out over the back of the lodge. The drop was steep—dangerously so—and it was obvious the entire backside of the building was built into the side of the mountain. Rachel was right. The space they were in now was far too small to account for the full size of the lodge. There had to be more. If not another room, then at least a crawl space. Tenner could be in there.

"There is nothing else," Matthew said flatly. "This is it."

"No. That's not possible. There *has* to be more. Look where this wall ends," Rachel insisted, pointing toward the wall behind the laundry machines. Then she pointed upward. "That might be the stairs above us—or more likely, it's still part of the great room. Think about how big it is up there."

Mia turned slowly, trying to piece together the basement's layout in her mind, to match it with the floor plan of the main level. But her focus slipped.

Ana was standing at the top of the stairs.

Her eyes were locked on Mia, intense and urgent. And Mia knew, without question, that Ana was trying to communicate. She'd seen flashes of spirits before, flickering in and out of reality, but never anything this clear. Normally, when she looked directly at them, they vanished. But not Ana. Ana held steady, solidifying with each sighting, her gaze pleading.

"Is there a closet down here?" Rachel asked, scanning the room. The brothers looked around, unsure. It was just one big open space—or so it seemed.

"Move the machines away from the wall," Rachel ordered. "Look for a door, or part of the wall that looks recently repaired. Anything."

The boys jumped into action, grunting as they worked together to slide the heavy appliances away from the wall, inch by inch.

Mia caught Rachel's eye, then glanced at the stairwell. Ana hadn't moved.

She was waiting.

Without a word, Mia turned and bolted, bounding up the stairs. Rachel's voice faded behind her as she left the basement—and their search—behind.

CHAPTER FIFTY-NINE

Mia Johnson

NOVEMBER, 2024

By the time Mia reached the top of the stairs, Ana was gone.

She hurried into the kitchen, only to find it empty—just a sink full of dirty dishes from dinner. She pushed through the swinging door and froze. Ana was standing in the middle of the great room.

This time, Mia didn't run. She stepped toward her slowly.

But with each step forward, Ana seemed to glide two steps back—without moving her feet. Before Mia knew it, she was standing in the lobby, staring up at the top of the staircase where Ana now stood, shrouded in shadow.

"Mia? Are you okay?"

Not Ana. Valentina.

She hadn't noticed the resemblance before now.

Before Mia could respond, the door to her parents' room creaked open. Her groggy parents squinted into the dim hallway light.

"Tenner is missing," Mia said, voice hollow. "We've looked everywhere."

The fog of sleep vanished in an instant. All three adults rushed down the stairs.

"Where's Rachel?" David demanded.

"She's with the guys. They're searching the basement."

Valentina crossed herself and sprinted toward the kitchen. Mia watched as she pushed through the swinging door, wondering how much of the lodge's haunted history Valentina actually knew.

Had she heard the stories? Did she believe them?

Mia turned back to find her parents already zipped into thick snow jackets that didn't belong to them—probably borrowed from the coat rack—and jamming their feet into boots.

"We're going outside to look," David said, reaching for the door.

"We already checked. There were no footprints. He couldn't have left the lodge," Mia protested, placing her hand firmly on the door.

"If you really searched the whole house," Lisa said, rummaging behind the reception desk and pulling out two flashlights, "then we *have* to check outside. The snow could've covered the prints. Or maybe the ice was thick enough that he didn't sink through. Either way, he could freeze out there."

Lisa was always disturbingly calm in an emergency. Her voice was flat, almost emotionless—cold logic over panic. "If anyone finds Tenner, have one of the boys sound the air horn so dad and I know to head back."

Mia lowered her arm and stepped back. She watched them trudge off into the dark, their boots sinking deeper with every step.

She closed the door behind them. Standing out there, freezing, wouldn't help anyone.

When she turned, Ana was behind the reception desk, her ghostly features tight with concern.

Mia rushed toward her, but caught her toe on the corner of the desk and stumbled forward with a yelp. She grabbed her foot, squeezing the aching toe, breath hissing through her teeth. When she looked up—Ana was gone. Again.

Mia sat down on the foldaway bed that had been pushed against the wall. She let herself cry.

She was glad to be alone. The last thing she needed was for Rachel to see her like this—to know she was capable of emotion.

"Tenner, where are you?" she whispered, choking back a sob. She leaned her head against the wall—

—and the bed rolled forward on its wheels.

Thrown off balance, Mia toppled sideways, scrambling to catch herself. Something slipped from her hoodie pocket, landing with a muted *ting* beneath the bed.

She reached into her hoodie pocket and pulled out a poker chip. Green. She leaned down to retrieve the one that had fallen—

—and froze.

There was a break in the molding at the center of the wall. Her eyes followed it upward, tracing a barely visible crack in the drywall.

Slowly, she stood. Pressed her palm against the wall.

It gave slightly, then bounced back—like a spring-loaded panel.

A hidden door.

Mia pressed again. This time, it popped open.

Revealing a dark, waiting doorway behind.

CHAPTER SIXTY

Rachel Johnson

NOVEMBER, 2024

Rachel felt the invisible tether between her and Mia tighten as her sister fled the basement. The guys had finished moving everything away from the walls and were now running their hands slowly along the surface, inch by inch, searching for seams or anything out of place.

She glanced toward the stairs, tempted to run after Mia—then remembered the door.

"Can that door be opened?" Rachel asked.

Matthew straightened and walked over to the large, roll-up door, leaving his brothers to continue searching. He grabbed the handle, and pulled hard.

Nothing. It didn't budge.

"Ice," he muttered. "The door can freeze shut."

Jon and Manny walked over to help when Matthew noticed the latch was still in place. He slid it over and gave one more powerful tug—and this time, the door rolled up with the smooth ease of something used every day—without the expected *loud-as-hell* noise.

Rachel stepped forward and looked out into the snow-covered landscape. Not a single footprint in sight.

She backed up to let Matthew close the door—then something caught her eye. A large drift of snow off to the side.

"What's that?" she asked, pointing.

"Sometimes the wind blows snow into big piles. Happens all the—" Matthew stopped mid-sentence as a chunk of snow slid from the tree above, revealing a patch of rusted red metal beneath.

"That's Murdoch's car," Manny said quietly from behind them.

"But he left days ago," Matthew said, frowning.

"No way he could've driven up in this storm," Jon added.

Rachel took a step back, the blood draining from her face. "Oh my God," she whispered. "He never actually left."

Panic gripped her as she turned and bolted up the stairs, tripping only once before catching herself. She flew through the kitchen, tore across the great room, and burst into the lobby, skidding to a stop at the base of the staircase where Valentina was hysterically yelling into the reception phone.

"Mia?" Rachel called out.

No answer.

Valentina slammed the phone down and stormed over to her boys as they rushed into the great room.

Rachel backed up, peeking into the game room. Empty.

Heading back toward the stairs—convinced Mia had gone to the upstairs bathroom—something in the office behind the reception desk caught her eye.

The wall.

It was open.

She crept around the desk, not even sure why she was moving so quietly. But her breath slowed, and her steps softened. The far wall stood ajar, revealing a dark, gaping void behind it.

"Mia?" she called again, voice trembling. She took a cautious step closer.

Behind her, the three brothers arrived, falling silent as they looked over her shoulder—staring into the blackness beyond the hidden doorway.

Chapter Sixty-One

Ella Whitmore

October, 2024

After a day in Murdoch Manor, Ella was already considering extending her stay. She was able to drift in and out most of the rooms without notice but there were still areas she had yet to search.

Theo—as Mr. Murdoch insisted she call him—had prepared a light meal that made her question whether he'd ever cooked before. If this place was going to survive, he was going to need staff.

She watched as Theo's car disappeared down the long driveway. He told her upon her arrival that he lived in the village below and could come back up if she needed anything. She'd reassured him that wouldn't be necessary—while silently celebrating the idea of having the entire place to herself. Finally, she could search for answers.

To be safe, she gave herself an extra two hours in case Theo returned for something he forgot. When she was confident he was truly gone, she made her move.

She'd declined the wine he offered with dinner, afraid it would make her drowsy. Not that it mattered—there was so much adrenaline in her veins she doubted she'd sleep for days.

When the time was right, she slipped her credit card into the master bedroom door and popped the lock.

Even with Theo gone, she had to be careful. Everything she touched had to go back *exactly* the way she found it. The lodge didn't appear high-tech, but she couldn't be sure there weren't cameras somewhere.

She eased the door closed behind her and took in the room. The bed was perfectly made—military-grade precision. The decor matched the rest of the lodge: rustic and haphazard.

Was this actually another guest room? Or had it always been locked because it belonged to the owner?

Ella moved cautiously across the room, pausing when a floorboard groaned beneath her foot.

She opened the first drawer. Empty.

She crossed to the dresser. Same result.

A sinking feeling gripped her gut.

Was this all just a massive waste of time? A wild goose chase built on nothing but ghost stories and town gossip?

Had she fallen for a marketing ploy?

As she turned toward the door, defeated, her hand brushed over the closet knob.

Locked.

Her pulse spiked.

Hope flickered.

She reached into her back pocket and pulled out her credit card, but the frame was too snug—there wasn't enough space between the door and the molding.

Thinking fast, she pulled the hairpin from her bun, straightened the metal, and yanked off the plastic tip, letting it fall to the floor. She slid the bare pin into the lock and jiggled it.

Click.

The door swung open—

Empty.

Her heart dropped.

She crumpled to the floor as tears welled in her eyes.

She had failed. Again.

First, she'd blown her big assignment. Not only had she come back without a story, but she'd landed herself on probation. And now—this. Chasing a rumor that probably started with some horny teenager looking for an excuse to get a girl back to his dorm.

And it led her to this: an empty closet in a forgotten manor on a forgotten mountain.

"Why?" she whispered, choking on the word. *Why lock the door if there was nothing inside?*

She'd already checked the other rooms on the landing. They were closed, but unlocked. So why this one? And why lock the closet?

She wiped away a tear, blinking to refocus—and then she saw it.

A dull metal latch on the closet floor.

Ella leaned forward, fingers brushing the faint outline of a square surrounding it. She looped one finger under the latch and pulled. A hidden panel popped up, and she rested it carefully against the back wall.

Beneath it, in the dark, lay a stack of old papers, filling the hidden space.

She reached in, hands trembling.

The first page was a laminated newspaper clipping dated 1975. The headline read: "Elias Thornfield and His Mountain of Torture?"

Ella's heart pounded in her ears.

This was it. *Paydirt.*

She pulled out her phone and began snapping photos as fast as she could. Each page held more history, more secrets. She didn't have time to read it all now—she'd do that at home.

Right now, she had one job: get the evidence—and get out.

CHAPTER SIXTY-TWO

Mia Johnson

NOVEMBER, 2024

Mia walked in a trance to the bottom of the staircase. She had found the hidden section of the basement. Turning to face the room, she froze in horror at the sight of a dungeon-like cell pressed against the far wall.

Her eyes swept the space. She was alone—except for a body slumped against the wall inside the cell.

Mia rushed forward, gripped the iron bars, and shook them. "Tenner! Wake up!"

The cell was locked, and no amount of rattling would break it open. Spinning around, Mia searched the room. The same bare concrete covered the floor and walls as in the adjacent space. Aside from the cell, only a single desk sat against the wall. And behind it, Ana stood.

Ana's gaze drifted down toward the desk, then back up to Mia.

Mia ran over. The desktop was bare, so she yanked drawers open. The center drawer held nothing but paper and worn pencils. She tugged open

231

the top left—inside lay two smashed cell phones and, beside them, a soft pink notebook. Mia's breath caught. She looked up at Ana, but the girl showed no reaction to what Mia knew had to be her journal.

Mia moved to the right and pulled the drawer so hard it toppled free, spilling its contents across the cold floor. Paper clips, batteries, coins—and a large, old key.

She seized it and sprinted back to the cell. Though the cage, lock, and key both looked rusted and ancient, the key slid in and turned smoothly. The door creaked open.

Tenner was cold to the touch, but breathing. Mia crouched beside him and tried to lift him, but he was dead weight, far too heavy even with adrenaline coursing through her. "Tenner, wake up!" she begged. When he didn't stir, she slapped him hard across the face.

"The air you breathe in a train station is fifteen percent skin."

His eyes flew open, then drooped shut again. A faint smile touched his mouth—enough to give Mia hope.

"I need you to stand. I can't get you out on my own," she pleaded, her teeth beginning to chatter.

"I... can't move." His words slurred.

"Yeah, dummy. You locked yourself in a dungeon. It's an icebox down here—you're lucky you didn't freeze."

"Murdoch," Tenner mumbled as he sagged lower. "He's been torturing... murdering people."

"No, not Murdoch," Mia protested quickly. "Some other guy—Thornfield—used the hotel for that, but it was ages ago."

"Murdoch..." Tenner's lips barely moved. "Is Thornfield's grandson."

The chill that swept over Mia had nothing to do with the basement air. "What are you talking about? How would you even know that?"

"I broke into his room. Files—in the closet. It's him. He drugged me... locked me in here. And I wasn't the first. There's blood... fresh blood. He's carrying on his grandfather's work."

The last words rasped out in a whisper before his eyes closed completely.

Mia's pulse thundered. She needed help. But she couldn't leave him—not with Murdoch still out there. She turned toward Ana, wondering if the girl could somehow intervene.

Before she could even meet her gaze, something slammed into her from behind. She crashed to the floor—her head landing hard against Tenner's leg instead of the concrete by some miracle. A small mercy.

It didn't last.

Theo Murdoch pinned her down, spider-like fingers coiling around her throat. He squeezed.

Tenner lay motionless, already unconscious again. Mia clawed at Murdoch's arms, then grabbed his wrists with both hands. Her fingers could encircle them completely, yet his height and wiry strength gave him an unshakable leverage.

Her lungs burned. Her nails raked at his skin, but nothing loosened his grip. Out of the corner of her eye, she saw Ana rush forward—only to stop dead at the cell's threshold. Her gaze dropped to the floor, then lifted back to Mia, her expression twisted with agony.

She could go no farther. Whatever horrors had claimed her in that very cell still frightened her—even in death.

Mia's vision tunneled. Black gauze seemed to drape across her sight. And the last thing she saw was the shimmer of a single tear sliding down Ana's translucent cheek.

CHAPTER SIXTY-THREE

Ella Whitmore

NOVEMBER, 2024

Ella sat curled up in the corner of her cell, staring past the cold, iron bars to the stairs across the room. When she first woke in what would become her torture chamber, she was happy to be alive. She was sure when her captor had wrapped his hands around her neck, that she'd taken her final breath. Her excitement at having another chance at life was short when she spotted the bars keeping her contained.

She had no idea how much time had passed since he first locked her in. Sometimes he came to her when small amounts of light came through the small dingy windows. Other times, he came in the dead of night when she couldn't even see her hand in front of her face. The first time he unlocked the cell, she fought back. Without a moment of indecision she threw herself at him. The shock on his face was a sure sign he didn't expect the attack and he threw hot wax from his candle at her, burning one eye.

The man was tall but frail and she knew she was stronger. But, starvation, dehydration, and bitter cold wore her down. She'd begun to wonder if he'd ever come back or if she would die in the cold dungeon all alone. When he finally returned, he came prepared, toting a lead pipe. Not that he needed it—her fight was gone. He opened her cell, dropped what looked to be cat food and a bowl of water on the ground, and as she scampered forward hit her in the arm with a solid blow from the lead pipe.

Each visit since, he brings food, water, and a beating. Hope was lost.

Until Ella heard more voices. New guests were upstairs. She tried to yell but after yelling so much upon her capture, her vocal cords could do little more than moan. When it was quiet at night and the people upstairs were more likely to hear, she moaned and cried hoping some sound would reach them.

As Ella prepared for another night of making whatever noise she could, she heard footsteps on the stairs to the basement. She jumped up with energy she no longer thought she had. Her excitement quickly drained when she saw it was her captor. He carried what looked to be a blanket and for a moment she wondered if the cruel, violent man had a change of heart.

When he reached the bottom, he spread the blanket out on the ground, picked up his lead pipe, and came at her.

She knew she wouldn't be saved.

CHAPTER SIXTY-FOUR

Rachel Johnson

NOVEMBER, 2024

Rachel flew down the stairs with the uncharacteristic grace of a ballerina and the speed of a sprinter. The sounds of struggle echoed below, and instinct took over—she ripped the fire extinguisher from its mount as she passed.

One glance was all it took: Mia was on the floor, a man's hands locked around her throat, and Tenner lay motionless nearby. Rachel didn't slow. She didn't hesitate. Blind courage surged through her veins as she charged forward, the brothers pounding down the steps close behind.

Hoisting the extinguisher high, she sprinted straight through a pocket of air so frigid it made her bones ache. The shiver that rattled her body only fueled her. With a raw, primal scream, she swung and brought the heavy metal crashing down on the back of Murdoch's skull.

The impact sent him sprawling. Rachel dropped to her knees beside Mia, gasping for breath herself. "Mia! Oh my gosh—are you okay? Breathe, please!"

Mia's chest heaved as a rasping cough broke free. Relief surged through Rachel, but she quickly turned to Matthew. He was crouched over Tenner. Their eyes met, and his small smile and slight nod told her everything—he was alive. She exhaled shakily.

"Let's get them out of here," Matthew barked to his brothers.

Jon dragged Murdoch's limp body to the corner of the cell, then rushed back to help Manny haul Tenner up. Together, they carried him toward the stairs.

CHAPTER SIXTY-FIVE

Mia Johnson

NOVEMBER, 2024

It hurt to swallow, and Mia couldn't make a sound. As Rachel and Matthew carried her out of the cell, she reached out. Her hand slipped straight through Ana's translucent form, but her arm caught on one of the iron bars.

Ana's gaze dropped to the cell door, the key still lodged in the lock.

"What, Mia?" Rachel snapped, breathless. "We need to get you upstairs."

Mia weakly pointed toward the door. Rachel understood instantly.

Matthew took Mia's full weight while Rachel swung the door shut and turned the key. The lock clanged shut, and Rachel pocketed it. Mia felt like a rag doll in Matthew's arms, her body limp and useless. Through the blur of her vision, she saw Rachel glance back at her, eyes brimming with tears.

"You did it, Mia," Rachel whispered, pride breaking through her trembling voice. "You saved him."

Matthew shifted her in his arms and started toward the stairs, granting Mia one last glimpse of Ana. A radiant smile spread across the ghost's face as she mouthed the words *thank you*—before Rachel's body passed right through her.

"The average person walks past thirty-six murderers in their lifetime," Mia rasped.

She shut her eyes, fighting tears, grieving the loss of someone she had never truly known.

Chapter Sixty-Six

Rachel Johnson

November, 2024

All Rachel wanted was to sit between Mia and Tenner, a hand on each of them, to reassure herself they were safe. But Mia insisted on her usual chair, and Tenner sprawled across the couch, forcing Rachel to perch awkwardly at his feet.

Valentina hadn't stopped moving—ducking in and out of the kitchen, heating blankets, fixing sandwiches, and bringing endless mugs of hot chocolate.

The front door banged open. Jon stomped inside, yanking his scarf from around his face and tossing it onto the coat rack. "I walked all the way out to the main road and blew the air horn until it was empty. Pretty sure I scared off every animal on this mountain, but trust me—they had to have heard it."

"Your parents should be back soon," Valentina told Rachel, though her strained face betrayed her doubt. She quickly turned back to the kitchen.

A rough cough from Tenner silenced the room. All eyes turned to him, though no one dared speak. He'd been through too much already, but they all wanted answers.

"Stop staring," he snapped. "I'm not broken."

Their gazes fell away, granting him the privacy he demanded.

"Look, I don't remember anything bad happening, okay?"

If he meant to reassure them, he failed. Rachel exchanged a look with Matthew but held her tongue.

"I told Matthew to let me search alone. It wasn't his fault."

Rachel gave a small nod. She hadn't blamed Matthew.

"I broke into Murdoch's room." He flicked his eyes toward Rachel, bracing for a scolding. "I know, I know."

She stayed quiet, waiting him out.

"Anyway, the room looked like every other guest room—bare, no personal stuff, no photos. Nobody had been staying there, so I took my time. I noticed the lock on the door looked broken—as if it had been tampered with—so I investigated."

Rachel's head was spinning as pieces of the puzzle came together. Ella's journal. When she wrote that she *broke in*, she must have meant into Murdoch's room, not into the hotel.

"It appeared that the closet was empty until I saw what I thought was a coin on the floor.," Tenner continued. "But, when I bent to pick it up, I realized it was a latch, like the one Mia found."

Tenner paused with a dramatic flair that was unexpected after what he'd experienced. "But, unlike the hidden space in Mia's room, it was full of documents."

Rachel couldn't hold back. "Why didn't you come get us? We could've looked at it together."

"Like I said, the place looked empty. We all saw Murdoch leave, right? And the more I flipped through the files, the clearer it became they were his. With him gone, what was there to worry about? If Valentina had found me, she would've what—told Mom and Dad? Please. They checked out the minute we got here."

Rachel pressed her lips tight, forcing herself to stay quiet. Mia's raspy voice broke the silence instead. "What did you find?"

"There were old newspaper clippings about the guy who used to run this place."

"Thornfield," Manny said.

"Right. You already know some of it. He lured people here, tortured them, then dumped their bodies off the cliff." A twisted smirk tugged at Tenner's mouth. "Guess those weren't all deer bones after all."

Rachel shot him a sharp glare, and the smirk vanished.

"Clipped to the front of the newspapers was an invoice—for a company called Web Erasure. No way it's legit. From what I could tell, they're hackers who scrub data from the internet. The bill was for a hundred grand. My guess? Those clippings are the last proof left of Thornfield's crimes. Erasing history doesn't come cheap."

"How do you know they were related?" Mia rasped.

"Who?" the others said in unison.

"Yeah," Tenner said, leaning forward. "Thornfield fathered a daughter, Cynthia with one of his first guests. She and her mom moved west, and he never saw them again. But decades later, when he was arrested, Cynthia was pregnant with her first child. Horrified at finding who her father really was, she gave her baby up for adoption."

"Let me guess," Matthew said grimly. "Murdoch."

Tenner nodded. The mountaintop lodge had been terrorized by not one, but two generations of killers for seven decades.

"So how'd Murdoch get the lodge?" Jon asked.

"The file had everything—birth certificates, adoption papers, death records. Thornfield died in prison, leaving the place to Cynthia. She never set foot here and died of cancer a couple years ago. The state tracked down Murdoch as the heir before the records were wiped."

"Wait—how the hell did you piece all this together?" Rachel asked, incredulous.

"You're not the only one good at puzzles." Tenner winked, some of his energy returning. "Remember, I was in that room for hours. I had plenty of time." His face darkened. "Honestly, I don't know what happened after that."

He rubbed the back of his head, wincing. "All I know is I woke up in that dungeon with a splitting headache, unable to stay awake. Never even saw him until you came down."

Tenner's eyes found Mia, softening with gratitude. "To save me."

CHAPTER SIXTY-SEVEN

Mia Johnson

NOVEMBER, 2024

The front door swung open, and Mia jolted upright. She thought the ache was only in her throat, but the sharp twist of her neck told her otherwise. She slid her hand up beneath the blanket and rubbed the tender spot, the plush fabric warm and soothing against her raw skin.

Lisa slammed the door shut, snow scattering from her boots as she kicked them off. She'd barely shrugged one arm free of her jacket when her eyes fell on Tenner sprawled on the couch. Her face lit up. She dashed across the foyer in wet socks, shedding her hat and gloves as she went, a trail of melting snow behind her. Reaching over the back of the couch, she wrapped Tenner in a fierce hug.

"Ew, Mom, you're soaked!" Tenner protested.

"He's still recovering, Lisa. Don't give him hypothermia. Change first, then smother him with warm hugs," Mia muttered, her raspy voice sharper than she intended.

Lisa froze, her gaze flicking toward Mia, studying the strained voice and unguarded expression of her youngest daughter. "What happened to you?" she asked softly.

"Where's Dad?" Rachel cut in.

Lisa straightened, scanning each face in the room as though searching for an answer in their eyes. Her arms fell slack at her sides, water pooling at her feet. "He... he's not here?"

"What? No!" Mia's voice cracked as she forced the words past her aching throat. "He left with you. You both left together. Where is he, Lisa?"

Cold fear coiled in her stomach, rising like ice through her chest until it froze her in place. She wanted to leap up, to rush to the door, to scream for her father—but her body refused to move.

Then, as suddenly as a light flicking on, Lisa's face shifted into a breezy smile. "I'm sure he's right behind me. He's fine. We split up—two flashlights cover more ground. I was pretty far out when I heard the air horn, so I turned back. He doesn't move as fast as me, so maybe I beat him back here." Her tone was light, casual. But the flicker in her eyes betrayed her words, and Mia felt the chill tighten its grip. Lisa wasn't nearly as certain about her husband's safety as she wanted them to believe.

Chapter Sixty-Eight

Rachel Johnson

November, 2024

Rachel awoke to a faint tickle across her forehead. Blinking her eyes open, she discovered it was the fine hairs on Tenner's feet brushing her face.

"Gross!" she yelped, springing to her feet.

Chairs scraped and blankets shifted as bodies stirred across the floor, startled awake by her outburst. For a moment, the chaos of limbs and yawns blurred together—until the sight of them all scattered across the great room brought the memory crashing back. They weren't just sleeping. They were waiting.

And the morning light spilling faintly through the trees confirmed the truth none of them wanted to voice. Their father still hadn't returned.

Rachel swallowed hard, fighting the lump rising in her throat. At the window, Valentina sat rigid in one of the dining chairs, her eyes fixed on the pale dawn outside. She hadn't moved, not even to glance back. Had she even slept?

Rachel's gaze swept the room, panic surging when she didn't see her mother—until she spotted her in the game room, mirroring Valentina's vigil from a second window.

Enough. Rachel couldn't sit there anymore. Maybe Dad had taken shelter in a hunting cabin, waiting for daylight. Maybe he'd made it down to town and couldn't get back up the icy road. She clung to those maybes as she rushed to the lobby, yanking the heavy rotary phone from its cradle.

The dial tone mocked her and her optimistic theories. If he'd found safety, someone would have called. The phone wasn't ringing—but not because the storm had cut the lines.

Her mother's wet jacket still lay discarded on the floor, but Rachel bypassed it, grabbing Jon's oversized coat from the rack instead. The thick fabric swallowed her whole, and she wondered if something so massive could even keep her warm.

"What are you doing?" Matthew's voice was low, careful, as if speaking too loudly might break her.

Her breaths came fast and shallow, chest rising in jerks. She knew if she didn't slow down, she'd hyperventilate.

"We need to look for him," she whispered, her voice splintering.

Matthew cupped her face gently, tilting it toward him, but before he could speak, Valentina's sharp cry cut through the room.

"Plow!"

Everyone rushed to the windows. A snowplow crawled up the drive, its scoop lifted, pressing the snow down more than clearing it. Behind it lumbered an ambulance, and at the rear, a sheriff's car crept forward before halting at the sign. The plow had cleared the main road, but snow coating the gravel drive was too treacherous for the low-clearance patrol car..

Jon broke from the group, tugging on his boots in the lobby before stepping out onto the porch. From inside, the family could only hear muffled voices, Jon speaking in hushed tones to a deputy. Rachel leaned closer, straining to catch a word, but her attention snagged on her mother—still unmoving in the game room.

She looked exhausted. Broken. As if even a blink might erase the scene outside—and with it, her husband.

The front door creaked open, and Jon ushered the emergency workers into the great room, the deputy and an officer toward the hidden basement stairs. Closing the door behind them, he faced the group.

"The deputy and his patrolman are taking Murdoch into custody. Search and rescue is on the way. The storm's passed, the sun's up, and the snow should start to melt soon."

The paramedics split, one examining Tenner, the other coaxing a fight from Mia. "If your epiglottis fails, you could suffocate," she warned, as they attempted to check her throat.

Jon's gaze flicked from Mia, to Tenner, and finally landed on Rachel. His voice carried the weight of a promise—and a plea.

"They'll find him."

CHAPTER SIXTY-NINE

Mia Johnson

LATE NOVEMBER, 2024

Jon was right.

They found him.

It only took a two-man rescue team an hour. But they found him.

David's body lay at the bottom of a cliff. *The* cliff.

It had been dark when he and Lisa set out to search for Tenner. David had simply been the unlucky one who headed the wrong way. He probably hadn't even realized he'd stepped off the edge until it was too late.

When the team descended to recover his body, they discovered another lying beside him—wrapped tightly in a blanket, frozen solid. The time of death was still uncertain, but the identification was immediate: Ella Whitmore, the missing journalist.

Mia's stomach twisted. The cries she and Rachel had heard those first nights in the lodge hadn't been in their heads. They belonged to Ella, trapped in the dungeon. And what Mia had glimpsed through her window *had* been Murdoch—carrying Ella's cocooned body into the woods.

As they waited on edge, through the recovery efforts, Mia told the brothers about Ana's journal, though she left out the part about seeing her ghost. The journal had been warning enough, its words preparing them for the grim confirmation the police investigation would bring.

Beneath Ella's frozen form, scattered in the snow, were more bones. At a glance, the group had once assumed they were deer remains, the ones spotted on their first hike. But up close, the truth was undeniable—many were human.

The rescue team recovered enough to identify Ana Miller, though several of her bones were missing, likely dragged off by animals.

Finally, Ana received justice, and her family found closure.

Chapter Seventy

Ana Miller

July, 2023

Ana Miller's life changed from dream-come-true to nightmare in a matter of months. Armed with her father's legal settlement, her family was positioned to buy and renovate the aging lodge on the mountaintop. The plan was perfect and her entire family would contribute. Ana and her mother, Valentina had the culinary and organizational skills to manage the mountain escape. Her father, who Ana was certain was on the road to recovery, would maintain the facility and grounds with Jon and Matthew. Manny, despite his introverted nature, was already showing signs of marketing genius.

When all the pieces were falling in place, her father's health took a turn for the worse he passed suddenly and way too soon.

With the lodge far from her mind, Ana mourned her father. But, on the eve of the public auction for the long-abandoned lodge, a distant heir was located and awarded the property.

Always the optimist, Valentina took the job to manage the lodge when it reopened under new management, certain the property would turn over again. Without consulting them first, Valentina hired her children to work for her.

Ana was infuriated. Why would they work as servants in someone else's lodge when they could build their own? She spent nights roaming the woods, writing in her journal, hitting trees with broken limbs—anything to vent her rage.

One night, her emotions boiled over before she could control herself. She pushed her mom. Hard. Valentina fell to the floor—blood trickled down her nose. But, it wasn't the blood that spooked Ana. It was the disappointment and worse—the fear she'd seen on her mother's face. She couldn't face what she'd done, so she ran.

Shame kept Ana away from home for several days. She'd slipped into the lodge through a broken window. The lodge that was supposed to belong to her family.

Ana spent hours writing in her little pink journal. What began as rage-writing, eventually shifted to gratitude journaling. She loved her family and would do anything for them—with them. Even if that meant working for someone else. Before her eyes shut on the third night, Ana made up her mind to return home the following morning. As she drifted off, hoping she had not caused her family too much anguish, the sound of a loud vehicle brought her fully awake. Peering out the second floor window, Ana watched a tall, lanky man exit a small, rusty car and walk towards the house.

Quietly creeping out to the balcony, Ana spied the man as he entered the foyer and disappeared into the room behind the reception desk. Minutes passed and the strange man had not reappeared. Curiosity got the better of her, and Ana tiptoed down the stairs. Though she did not find the man she was looking for, she did find a door against the back wall that she'd not previously seen.

The door led to a steep stairwell—dark with a musty odor. She descended the stairs and found herself alone in a basement, staring at what looked to be a medieval dungeon.

Ana stepped closer. A small candle on a desk illuminating only a small portion of the room—casting the rest in shadows.

Realizing she should be reaching out to the police rather than investigating the intruder on her own, Ana spun around only to find herself face-to-face with the tall man. She had to tilt her head backward to look him in the face, and what she saw was chilling. A smile.

"Please," Ana pleaded as a tear slid down her cheek. "I'm only sixteen."

Her desperate appeal only seemed to excite him more, as his smile spread even wider and he stepped closer, hoisting a led pipe over his head.

In that moment, Ana prayed her family would one day uncover the truth of her fate—however unbearable it might be. They needed closure... and her soul depended on it. Without answers, without justice, she knew she would be doomed to linger inside the cursed lodge, bound to its horrors for eternity.

CHAPTER SEVENTY-ONE

Rachel Johnson

JANUARY, 2025

"Hey." The familiar voice that once made her knees weak was a welcome break to her studies.

"Hey," Rachel responded.

"How are you doing?"

"Fine. you?"

"Fine."

When Rachel first met Matthew, the thought of him calling her after their vacation would have sent her heart racing. Back then, butterflies and nervous energy would have driven her to fill every pause with small talk, desperate to chase away the awkwardness.

But now—for the first time in her life—she didn't feel the need to say a word. She sat in the quiet, phone pressed to her ear, content knowing he was there on the other end of the line.

Matthew cleared his throat.

"How's Mia?"

""Broody, but that's her factory default."

"Tenner?"

"His grades have been dropping, not that he's ever cared much about grades before."

Before and after.

Their lives were now divided into two parts: before their trip to Murder Manor, and after. Before her brother was trapped and nearly murdered—and after. Before her father fell to his death from a cliff in the middle of the night, searching for his missing son, likely still half-drugged on migraine medication.

And after. After the roads were cleared. After Murdoch was arrested. After her father's body was recovered—and more were unearthed. After they came home and tried, piece by piece, to stitch their lives back together.

"He got into a fight with some kid at school. Probably should've been suspended, but the administration felt bad for him. The principal went to high school with my mom and dad back in the day."

"Rachel."

She knew that tone—calm but heavy—and that meant something serious was coming.

"You know you can talk to me about anything, right? You don't have to keep it all inside. I understand what it's like... to lose your father. You want to be strong for your mom and your siblings, but you need to take care of yourself too. You know that, right? I'm here for you."

Rachel nodded, careful not to speak. She knew he couldn't see her acknowledgment, but even a single word felt fragile, like it might shatter her core.

Silence stretched between them.

When they first returned home, Matthew called nearly every day. He never pushed her to relive what had happened, instead steering the conversation toward classes, volunteering, college applications, and other distractions—carefully avoiding the elephant in the room. Looking back now, Rachel appreciated how much that had helped. She hadn't been ready to talk about everything, and he had gently nudged her toward the future. Slowly, the calls had dwindled to texts, and the time between responses had stretched longer and longer.

Unlike her initial reaction to him, she now felt safe being herself. She didn't have to impress him, and the tension of potential romance had eased into the comfort of an old friend. Her first crush, it seemed, had quietly migrated to the friend zone.

Thanks, trauma.

"So," Matthew's voice cut through the quiet. "I'm actually calling because I have some information. I'm not sure you're ready for it, but I thought you should decide whether you want to hear it."

"Tell me," Rachel said, too quickly. "Look... we all saw a therapist. Mia and I—well, we graduated, so to speak. My dad died. It sucks. But I'm coping. The part that's driving me crazy is not knowing the answers to all the questions swirling in my head. That's the part I can't handle."

"Okay. I understand." Matthew paused, gathering himself, then continued.

"Most of what Tenner discovered has been confirmed. Thornfield built the Murder Manor to lure, torture, and kill. The guy was bat-shit crazy. A few years after opening the lodge, he had a daughter with a guest. I guess his baby-mama should consider herself lucky she was a one-night stand instead of a murder victim. She and her daughter, Cynthia Smith, were mostly estranged from him, moving across the country with very little contact. Cynthia became pregnant in her late teens, the year Thornfield was arrested. When she learned the full extent of his crimes, she gave her son up for adoption, afraid of who he might become."

"A family named Murdoch adopted him, despite a rare muscular deficiency he was born with. They seem to have been good people, but rather than deal with the relentless bullying he faced for his appearance, they ran—moving nearly every year. Now, with his DNA on file, authorities were able to link him to two murders from his time in Chicago back in 2007. The psychological profilers believe he targets children and slight women because it makes him feel strong."

"When Thornfield died in prison in '95, he left the lodge to Cynthia in his will. She never visited, sold, or used it in any way. She died from a long illness in 2022. Her estate was in probate, with no living relatives—but days before the lodge went to auction, a clerk tracked down the adoption records and located Murdoch, leaving him the sole beneficiary."

"The agent who took Murdoch up the mountain to hand over the deed thought it odd that he wanted to spend the night, even though the place was in total disrepair. Police believe he found the hotel's history—including his grandfather's dark past—before the visit, which likely inspired him to follow in Thornfield's footsteps."

"The investigators also think he hired hackers from the dark web to erase the lodge's history, but the company listed on the receipt doesn't exist. Of course."

"The police reviewed Ana's journal. They believe she had already been staying there when Murdoch arrived the first night. Her entries show she'd been sleeping in the abandoned lodge for at least a few nights before her writing stopped."

A long pause stretched between them. Rachel didn't interrupt—grateful for the information, but aware that revisiting these horrors was no small burden for him.

Matthew drew a deep breath, as though closing the story. But before Rachel could respond, he added, "Thank Mia for me. Please."

"For what?" Rachel asked softly.

"She told us about the journal before the police found it. Eventually, we turned it over, but reading it first was... therapeutic. The four of us sat together and read. Ana was angry. She was sad. But she loved us. Seeing that in writing gave us peace."

Rachel didn't know what to say. Matthew had been so supportive—checking in, sending memes to lighten her mood—but she had done nothing for him in return. Words of reassurance and empathy escaped her. Instead, she said, quietly, "I'll let her know."

She knew then that their conversations were over. Whatever their relationship had been, it had run its course. She wanted to thank him for being kind, for being her first crush, for always asking after her family—but the words wouldn't come.

"Thanks, Matthew."

"Anytime, Rachel. Bye."

He was gone. The line went dead, yet the phone remained pressed to her cheek.

"Goodbye," Rachel whispered.

CHAPTER SEVENTY-TWO

Mia Johnson

DECEMBER, 2026

Mia stepped out of the car onto the gravel drive, a smile tugging at her lips. The lodge—less the run-down relic from the last century she remembered, more a masterpiece of historical character with modern sophistication—looked radiant in the crisp winter sunlight. Holiday decorations sparkled across the porch: fresh green garlands wrapped around the railings, dotted with velvet red bows, and a large wreath crowned the front window. Mia exhaled, relieved not to see Ana's face staring back at her.

Her family raced ahead, carrying bags and laughing, their excitement bouncing off the freshly stained porch. Mia lingered a moment, taking it all in. Valentina had thrown herself into the remodel after the Murdoch investigation ended, hiring local craftsmen to restore every corner with care. If the lodge was to shed its dark reputation and become a beloved part of the community, it had to be a collective effort.

The lodge reopened over a year ago. Though Mia and her family had been invited as guests of honor, they declined, needing time to grieve and heal. Now, Valentina had reserved the week of Christmas for both families, welcoming them with open arms and a house glowing with warmth. Twinkling lights traced the eaves, the scent of pine and cinnamon wafted through the air, and snow lightly dusted the roof like powdered sugar on a holiday cake.

Manny, rarely a people person, had taken on the marketing himself—rebranding the lodge, Summit House. Rather than erase the lodge's past, he let the remodel shine. Photos circulated online, spreading viral buzz—not to glorify the tragedy, but to celebrate the lodge's new life. The mountain, the lodge, the snow-dusted trees—they were breathtaking. History had happened, yes, but it didn't define the present.

No sign of Ana appeared in the windows or at the door left wide-open by Tenner. Mia allowed herself a flutter of hope that Ana's spirit had finally found peace. She looked down the driveway, now edged with smooth stones gathered from the surrounding hills. Where previously, the drive up had been a broken axle waiting to happen—whether Valentina had paid to repair it or the city had taken over, the road was now smooth.

Mia breathed in the cold, clean mountain air, savoring the mix of pine, snow, and a touch of winter magic. She knew stepping inside would awaken memories she had buried, but the festive glow around her lent courage. The wreaths, garlands, and lights were like tiny shields against the shadows of the past, and she felt a small warmth bloom in her chest.

Steeling herself, she walked toward the lodge—only to freeze mid-step. There, bathed in sunlight glinting off the roof, was her father. For a heartbeat, she didn't see him at all. Then, as she took a second glance, his figure shimmered—soft, translucent, impossibly real—and vanished. Mia's heart seized with a mix of longing and fear.

Why hadn't David moved on? What was keeping his spirit here?

CHAPTER SEVENTY-THREE

Lisa Johnson

DECEMBER, 2026

Lisa was oddly comfortable being back at the lodge and seeing Valentina and the boys. They'd kept in touch over the years, but she hadn't seen them since their last visit. It was amazing to see what Valentina had done with the place. The lodge looked so transformed that Lisa wouldn't have blinked if someone had told her they tore it down and rebuilt it from scratch. From the floors to the furniture, lighting, and exterior landscaping, the lodge was the ultimate mountain retreat. True to Valentina's natural hospitality, she had stocked plenty of Lisa's favorite wine and kept her glass constantly filled.

If it weren't for Mia's occasional reminders, Lisa could hardly imagine that something so horrible had happened there just two years ago. You'd be surprised how many eerie facts exist about cliff deaths.

As the lodge had a rejuvenation—so had Lisa. Valentina barely recognized her with the new look. She'd trimmed down thanks to daily yoga and weekend pickleball, and her cut and color were more fashionable than ever.

Valentina's astonishment came as a surprise—none of her kids had commented on the change. Perhaps her weight loss was a subtle reminder of a difficult year, or maybe it wasn't polite to remark on someone's appearance in today's environment. Either way, Lisa felt lighter, not just physically, but spiritually. Her relationship with her kids was kinder, her energy higher, and she slept like a rock.

The past couple of years had been full of highs and lows, and they were all still adjusting to life without David. It was sad not having his presence, but she had to admit it was a lot less work. Caring for him for so long—though she loved him—had been exhausting and thankless.

Tenner found a connection with his new therapist and continued weekly sessions. He had endured a traumatic experience but came out physically unharmed, with only faint memories of the ordeal. He found a healthy outlet for his pent-up rage—cross country running. His grades improved too, though Lisa suspected that the motivation had more to do with eligibility to race than a newfound love of learning.

Mia's voice remained permanently raspy from damage to her vocal cords, yet in true Mia fashion, she embraced it, even suggesting that she might become a voice actor, using her unique tone for creepy storytelling.

Rachel graduated top of her class and was halfway through her freshman year at Princeton. She settled quickly, diving into studies while finding her people—students who worked hard but knew how to unwind. To everyone's surprise, she joined a flag football team and even had a boyfriend, Paul.

Of course, the kids missed their dad. Though none had voiced their feelings aloud—life without him was simpler—no more listening to complaints about constant headaches, no more interference in every decision or obsession with true crime. Taking care of him had been suffocating, a constant pressure she was glad to release.

There were benefits, however, to his true crime obsession. He would zone out for hours and listen to those damned podcasts. Lisa was never into true crime, but would often hear it in the background when he was listening without headphones or watching a documentary on tv.

If it wasn't for all her secondhand eavesdropping, she would never have had the dark, devious idea to exploit a serial killer on the loose—and give her husband a little push off the deadly cliff.

Thank You for Reading

If you enjoyed MURDER MANOR, please consider leaving an honest
review on your preferred platform.
Your feedback in invaluable and helps other readers discover new books
and authors.

If you didn't love it—sorry it wasn't your jam.
Thanks for giving me a try.

As fear takes hold, the family discovers they are completely cut off: no cell service, no internet, and the boat that brought them won't return for days.

The Unwelcome Guest bides his time, hiding in the walls, waiting for the perfect moment to strike while the family's dream vacation turns into a deadly nightmare they can't escape.

In **Making a Killing** by Cori Nevruz, Natalia thought she had finally escaped her mother's suffocating grip, only to be drawn into a web of dark family secrets. A quirky misfit, she heads to New York City, driven by the discovery of a stepbrother she never knew—Daniel. Desperate for love and acceptance, Natalia carefully molds herself into the perfect sibling he expects. But her hidden life tells a different story.

By day, Natalia works for Stuart, an eccentric corporate powerhouse, covertly eliminating retired pension recipients. With a knack for making each hit seem accidental or natural, she rationalizes her deviant actions by focusing on her victims' flaws. The pay is good, and her skills sharpen with each job, but the weight of her dual life starts to wear thin.

As Natalia spends more time with Stuart, his enigmatic wife, and a budding romantic partner, her carefully constructed facade begins to crumble. Daniel's growing suspicion forces Natalia into a dangerous balancing act. Can she maintain the illusion, or will her true identity be revealed, setting off a chain reaction that could shatter her newfound connections?

Making a Killing is a gripping tale of deception, identity, and the deadly cost of living a double life.

Left Without Answers by Cori Nevruz plunges readers into a heart-stopping journey of grief, mystery, and unyielding determination. After the sudden and unexplained loss of her son Hank, Alice is consumed by a relentless need for answers. The vibrant spirit of her boy couldn't just vanish without a trace—there must be more to the story.

As Alice reaches out to Hank's best friend Arnold, she's met with a chilling resistance. Arnold, like everyone else, insists she move on, urging her to let the past rest. But Alice's motherly intuition is a force that cannot be silenced, especially when she begins finding cryptic notes from Hank. Could Hank be reaching out from beyond, or is something more sinister at play?

Alice's quest leads her deep into Hank's hidden life, unraveling a web of betrayal, bullying, and secrets darker than she ever imagined. Each revelation threatens to tip her over the edge of sanity, as she battles the terrifying truths lurking in the shadows.

In a race against time and her own fears, Alice must uncover the truth behind her son's death. But as the specters of Hank's final moments haunt her, Alice faces a chilling realization—some secrets are meant to stay buried. Will her search for answers bring justice, or will it plunge her into a nightmare from which there is no escape?

Left Without Answers is a gripping, suspense-filled thriller that will keep you on the edge of your seat until the final page.

Dirty Laundry by Cori Nevruz invites readers into the fragile world of Samantha, a former perfectionist whose once-orderly life spirals into chaos with the addition of a husband and children. As the facade of her perfect suburban existence cracks, Samantha's insecurities deepen, fueled by her husband's relentless criticism and impossible expectations.

Beneath the surface of cheerful smiles and staged social appearances lies a woman teetering on the edge, her hidden turmoil spilling into the pages of a secret journal. But when Samantha confides in a new friend, her carefully constructed life unravels, exposing dangerous truths that threaten both their lives.

What dark secrets could shatter the illusion of Samantha's seemingly perfect life? **Dirty Laundry** is a fast-paced, suspenseful journey into the mind of a mom on the edge.

About the Author

Cori Nevruz is a suspense and thriller author in Wilmington, North Carolina [USA], where she balances her writing career with family life alongside her husband, three sons and two dogs, Chumply and Munch. When she's not crafting unhinged stories, she enjoys reading and passionately following her favorite sports.

Visit her website at http://CoriWroteABook.com.

www.ingramcontent.com/pod-product-compliance
Lightning Source LLC
Chambersburg PA
CBHW071503110726
47908CB00003B/711